A Little's Dreams Come True

Welcome Home, Baby Girl

+

We Will Never Leave You, Baby Girl

A DDLG and ABDL 2 in 1 novel collection of kinky BDSM age play stories

Tina Moore

Table of Contents

Welcome Home, Baby Girl

An MDLG, DDLG & ABDL novel about a Mommy & Daddy Dom who train their naughty girl to be the perfect little one

Tina Moore

Chapter 1

He finished buttoning up his crisp, white dress shirt but left the top buttons undone, exposing the smooth tan skin of his throat.

"Ready to go?" Liam asked, his voice thick with desire as he looked at his wife. Dressed in a gorgeous full-skirted dress and a pearl-string necklace, Josie cut quite a striking figure. They both loved getting dressed for these occasions. Josie gave him a suggestive wink, "Always." As she brushed past him, Josie deliberately squeezed the bulge in his pants.

***

The entranceway was decorated in muted colors. Liam and Josie shrugged off their coats and carefully handed them to one of the supervisors who carefully transferred them to the closet.

"Evening, Chelsey. How are you tonight?" Josie asked. The question was standard and had an underlying purpose: They needed to know if there were any potential troublemakers in the house today. Not everybody played well together.

"Good to see you two again," Chelsey glanced through the doorway to her left. "Brandon is in here tonight. I'm on coffee duty." As she said that a pair came out from where Chelsey had been motioning. The man was dressed in a beautiful navy blue suit and a crisp, white button-up. He was holding the hand of his Little, dressed in a yellow dress and holding a penguin stuffie under her arm, nodding as she talked animatedly. He nodded a greeting to Liam and sent a silent signal to Chelsey. The three of them quietly disappeared into an adjoining room where they could hear cups being prepared.

Liam and Josie stepped through the door, glancing around, greeting some of the other Daddies and Mommies they had come to know outside of this space. Josie kissed his hand, and he watched her disappear around the corner. She would go around the house, greeting everyone before finding somewhere to settle in.

It usually took Liam a while longer to get into the right headspace. Sometimes even longer if he had had a bad day in court, and today had been a *really* bad day. The opposition had put up a really strong defense, and the potential to lose his case was weighing heavily on him. Liam rarely lost, and the threat put him on edge. The anger wasn't welcome here, so he needed a moment to reset. Liam turned around and went through the door where the other couple and Chelsey disappeared a few heartbeats earlier. The kitchen was set up to be the neutral space. Nothing but coffee happened in there. You could walk in, grab a cup, and sit down. Even if that was all you did all night, it was a safe place, and the people were kind enough to pass no judgments. Chelsey had prepared a fresh pot of coffee and brought a cup over to where he sat on an ancient, wooden kitchen chair.

"Want to talk about it?" Chelsey prompted after passing him the tray with cream and sugar.

"Nah. Thanks, though, Chels. I appreciate the offer." Liam stirred absent-mindedly and listened to the couple as they talked about mundane things, drinking their coffee, and accepting Chelsey's offer of cookies. Liam drained his coffee, savoring the sweet, creamy residue at the bottom of the cup. He ran his hands through his hair and decided to head deeper into the house.

Liam did what he always did and stood in the doorway of the Little room, where a few little girls were coloring and laughing. He loved seeing them as happy as they were. Relaxed and content.

A few girls were wearing onesies, while others wore dresses and bows. The color alone made his heart swell. When he stepped inside, the girls looked up at him. One little girl with a large pink scrunchie holding her long dark hair tied above her head beamed a smile at him, waving ecstatically.

Liam went over and sat down next to her, "Hi, Ella, what are you working on today?"

"It's my favorite!" Ella held up her picture proudly. The page was full of butterflies, colored with every color imaginable. She had even signed her name in the bottom corner of the page.

"That's really good, angel. Can you draw something for me, too?" Liam asked.
Ella immediately complied and pulled out a blank sheet of paper.
When she was done, Liam carefully took the picture from Ella and held it up for inspection.

Good girl! This picture is absolutely beautiful." She beamed at him, and a flush crept up her neck and onto her cheeks.

"Thank you, Mr. Liam," Ella said shyly.

"Can I keep this one?"
Ella nodded and returned to her drawings.

"Thank you, Ella. Be a good little girl, okay?"

"I will, Mr. Liam."
With a gentle pat of her hand, Liam rose to his feet and left her to her own devices.
It was normal that some Littles would prefer to be in their little space simply. Coloring, snuggling and doing Little things. Just like anyone else wouldn't always be in the mood for

anything more serious than light petting, each Little had their own needs that changed from day to day and from moment to moment.

Liam passed Brandon as he wandered further into the house, who simply acknowledged his existence with a brief nod of his head before continuing his rotation. There were three supervisors throughout the house, aside from Chelsey. While nothing untoward happened, their existence was to ensure the safety and comfort of the people involved. Rules were in place for a reason, and newcomers weren't allowed to be part of the events if they did not agree to all of them.

From somewhere down the hall, Liam heard squeals of joy and hysterical laughter. He knew without needing to go see that it was one of the more salacious rooms. One he liked visiting himself; however, that particular experience would be saved for another time.

Liam found Josie on the couch with a Little snuggled up to her as they watched cartoons on a massive TV hanging on the opposite wall. Josie caught his eye and motioned for him to come over.

Liam gave Josie a kiss on the top of her head and whispered in her ear, "When you're ready, you know where to find me, Jo."

His voice was husky, and Josie felt heat pool between her legs. With Dylan snuggled so close to her, she could feel the muscles in his body tense and relax as he shifted to get more comfortable.

Josie knew Liam had already left. He didn't need an answer. She knew where to find him if she wanted to join him. Right now, she felt content and happy, holding Dylan close to her. While she didn't have her own Little, Dylan was more than eager to share himself with her whenever he could.

"Mommy?"

"Yes, little man?"

"Do you have to go with Mr. Liam now?"

Josie smiled and brushed the hair from his eyes, kissing the tip of his nose, "Of course not, sweetie. We don't have to go anywhere or do

anything that you don't want to, remember?"
Dylan nodded and was quiet for a while, his
attention on the purple dog on the TV screen.
After a short while, he looked up at Josie,
"Mommy?"

"Yes, sweetie?"

"Do you think Mr. Liam will want to be
my Daddy tonight?"
It took Josie by surprise, and perhaps it showed
on her face because Dylan scrunched his face up
and hastily added, "It's okay if he doesn't. It's
okay if you don't either, Mommy. I just-"
Josie put a gentle finger to his lips, still showing
no sign of anger or irritability, "We can go ask
him, Dylan. Are you sure that's what you want?"
Josie was serious. She had never seen Dylan
interested in anyone other than a handful of
other Mommies, and he seemed especially
withdrawn from Liam and the other Daddies
that frequented the play parties.

"You're not mad at me?" Dylan asked, a
catch in his voice.

"Of course not," Josie planted soft kisses

all over his face, making him giggle. "You're my sweet baby boy, how could I ever be mad at you?"

Dylan hopped off the couch excitedly, holding Josie's hand, "Can we go now, Mommy?"

"What's the magic word?"

"Please," Dylan laughed and bounced on the balls of his feet, dragging Josie behind him. As they entered the hallway, Josie gently pulled him to a stop, "Remember, there are other people here too, so we need to be quiet and respectful."

"Yes, Mommy."

The pair made their way through the house. Some doors were closed, and Josie heard the unmistakable sounds of sex coming from them. Behind another, the sharp crack as a paddle met bare flesh. The sounds made Josie lick her lips in anticipation.

They passed by a room that held four "cubicles," which were small safe spaces enclosed with heavy drapes hanging from the ceiling. The curtains were there if the Caregiver and Little needed a little privacy for their aftercare. Not everyone liked to be watched during such an intimate moment. The room was empty for now but would have occupants soon enough.

She felt Dylan hesitate as they neared the room in the back where Liam was sure to be. Josie stopped and pulled him to her, "You really don't have to do anything you don't want to, little man."

"I'm scared you'll be mad and never want to be my Mommy again."

Josie looked at him, reassuringly, "I promised that I would never lie to you, Dylan. And you promised me, too."

Dylan looked at the floor and in the softest voice, said, "I- I don't think I'm ready for that yet."

"It really is okay, Dylan," Josie stressed his name so he would look up at her. "We can go back and just snuggle on the couch exactly like we always do."

"Yes, please." Josie hugged him tightly and led him back to the TV room, "You don't have to do anything you don't want to."

Dylan nodded and looked at the floor as he hesitated in the doorway, his fingers still wrapped around hers, "Is it okay if I watch by myself for a little bit?"

"Whatever you want, little one." Dylan's mood instantly picked up again, and he leaped into her arms for a hug.

Josie gave Dylan one last big bear hug and helped him get comfortable on the sofa. She handed him his sippy cup and watched from the doorway as he settled himself in.

Josie was a bit disappointed, but she never wanted Dylan to do anything he wasn't ready for, so she didn't get angry. Josie accepted him for who he was and let him do what he needed. It was the same for everyone here. On the odd occasion, they would encounter a bad apple who soured the mood and experience for everyone, but the problems were resolved quickly and quietly.

The rules were there for a reason. No is no; no exceptions.

Josie hummed to herself as she walked back to

the drawing-room, needing to spend a little time with the girls before finding Liam.

"Josie!" an ear-splitting squeal of delight drew her attention to the doorway where a familiar face was impatiently handing off her coat and bag.

"Piper, sweetheart, how have you been?" Josie half-laughed as Piper ran up and nearly knocked her over as she threw her arms around Josie. A full head shorter than Josie, Piper's thin frame and large blue eyes made her look like a doll.

"Everything has been so much fun, Mommy!"
Josie couldn't stop smiling. Piper's laugh was infectious, and her bubbly personality lit up the room. The other Littles stared at her, giggling and whispering. Some even temporarily abandoned their artwork and clumped around the two of them. Piper made friends easily, and she adored the girls as much as they adored her.

****

Liam growled low in his throat, "Just like that, good girl Lexi."

It was one of the rare rooms that had their door open, given the explicit nature of what was happening within. There were two women at Liam's feet, still fully clothed, looking up at him expectantly. He had stripped naked for the scene, the muscles in his thighs working as he shifted his weight as the girls continued their instruction.

The one he called Lexi had a dark green training collar around her neck, and the lead was wrapped around Liam's muscular forearm. Lexi's full-time Daddy, Carlisle, was standing slightly to one side, watching the scene before him. He caught Josie's attention, and she quietly went in, Piper following close behind, her eyes locked on Liam's cock as the girls licked and suckled him. Josie recognized the other Little as Octavia. She didn't belong to anyone but, much like a lot of the girls at the party, preferred to have more than one Daddy. She generally went with what she felt in the mood for that day and fell in where they accepted her.

Carlisle motioned Josie over and whispered in her ear, "Liam's a good teacher. I have trained a lot of Littles, but he has that, special touch."

Josie couldn't help but notice the bulge in his jeans as his eyes darkened, watching as Liam carefully pulled Lexi closer by the lead, repositioning her for the next lesson.

Josie agreed with Carlisle; Liam was gentle and caring even when training and dealing with extremely bratty, little girls. She knew he secretly liked the fire in their eyes when they tried to defy him.

Josie's eyes wandered around the room and saw that there were a few other people also enjoying the scene. She desperately wanted to join in, especially since Piper was pressing herself against Josie in a way that made her acutely aware that she definitely wasn't a little girl underneath all those frills.

Liam glanced at Josie and Piper and held out his free hand to them. He glanced down at the two in front of him, and they gave the most subtle nod, consenting to the addition of two more to their group. Liam had made arrangements with Carlisle before they had started, and he had agreed to the addition.

Liam stood back, releasing the slack on the lead, and Lexi stood up demurely. She couldn't help but glance at Carlisle as he watched from the sidelines, an action Liam did not miss.

"Octavia, could you help Daddy undress, Lexi, please?"

"Yes, Daddy."

As Josie joined them, she beckoned to Piper, "Come here, pumpkin."

"But-"

The look Josie gave Piper stopped the words in her throat. She gave one lustful glance to Liam and walked into Josie's open arms, "I'm sorry, Mommy."

"You will get your turn, pumpkin. Daddy is busy teaching a new baby girl the rules."

"Did she talk back?" Piper asked, eyes wide, still watching the scene.

As Octavia unzipped Lexi's summer dress, they watched it fall to the floor. Her bottom was already a little red from where Liam had spanked her.

"Why don't you ask her, Piper?"

Piper bit her lip as did as instructed, "Little Lexi, why is Daddy punishing you?"

Her face flushed red, Lexi looked up at Piper, "I called Daddy a bad word. I'm not allowed to say bad words."

Liam had Lexi positioned on her knees in front of him, her bottom facing him. His cock jerked, but he knew she was not to be touched in that way. Those were the terms set by Carlisle. Liam pulled back his hand and, with a loud *whack,* made contact with her bare skin. Lexi squirmed and let out a small sound.

"What are the rules Carlisle has given you, Lexi?" Liam asked, his voice was hard but still gentle as he addressed her.

"I will not lie."

Whack.

"I will not backtalk or argue."

Whack.

"I will not use bad language."

Whack.

"I will do my chores."

Whack.

Liam softly rubbed over the stinging parts of her flesh, and Lexi let out a moan of pleasure. Her lips were swollen and moist.

Josie had discarded her dress, revealing her bare skin underneath. She enjoyed the thrill of going out into public with the added risk of exposing herself. It made her feel more powerful in a way.

"Kneel for me, please, pumpkin." Piper thought about resisting Mommy's commands but knew she would have more fun if she listened like a good girl. Octavia wasn't quite as shy as Lexi, but her face and ears still burned with embarrassment as she knelt next to Josie's prone form, "Mommy, can I... can I touch you please?"

Josie sighed with pleasure as Piper's lips met her inner thighs, and it took a heartbeat before she could answer, "You may do what you want

Octavia, as long as you do not disturb Daddy until he calls for you."

Octavia gave a squeal of happiness and quickly ran around to join Piper, her hands running up Josie's bare thighs to touch her core, "Is this okay, Mommy?"

"You're both doing very well, my darlings."

Piper giggled as Josie opened her legs wider to give both girls better access. Josie let out a moan as Octavia's fingers touched her core, causing goosebumps to erupt across her skin.

"What do we say when we've broken the rules, Lexi?" Liam prompted, massaging her red cheeks.

"I'm sorry, Daddy."

"And?"

Lexi pushed back against his hands, "But, Daddy-"

Whack. Whack.

He gave her two short, sharp smacks, and Lexi squealed, "I'm sorry, Daddy. I won't break the rules again."

"Good girl, Lexi," Liam said as he rubbed her ass again, his cock twitching as he watched the moisture spread and glisten in the light. Liam pulled on the lead, and Lexi came around to face him, still on all fours.

"Open."

Lexi obeyed, opening her mouth wide, her eyes dark with need but eager to please.

Liam pushed his cock into her mouth just as another couple entered the room to watch. He knotted his hand in her hair and tightened the lead with the other, "Keep your throat open, little one, and breathe through your nose."

Whenever Lexi gagged, Liam would pull back a little and whisper to her reassuringly, his cock growing harder as he listened to his wife's moans of pleasure. Precum leaked from his tip, and he pulled away from Lexi. His heart was hammering fiercely, and it took all of his willpower not to cum on her face.

"Did I do something wrong, Daddy?" Lexi asked, her voice soft and uncertain.

"No, little girl, you are doing very well."

Liam knelt down next to her and kissed her cheek, "Promise that you will try your very best to be a good girl?"

"I promise, Daddy."

Liam helped her to her feet and scooped her up. Lexi's small frame made it incredibly easy for him to carry her around. He nodded to Carlisle, and the three of them left the room. Liam settled onto one of the couches in the curtained room with Lexi on his lap as Carlisle closed the curtain to afford them a little privacy.

"You were such a good girl, Lexi. I'm very proud of you."

Lexi tucked her head beneath his chin and listened to his heartbeat, "Thank you, Daddy."

Chapter 2

Liam and Josie had hosted their share of play parties, but if they were truly honest with themselves, they preferred to attend rather than host. While hosting had the benefit of setting the mood and providing indirect care for everyone involved, they preferred to be in the thick of things. Not on the sidelines.

Liam and Josie had taken a shower together. Instead of arriving late as they had thought, Liam and Josie were one of the first of the guests at the party this time. It was a new group of people and happened to be facilitated by a different couple. They had attended nearly every party each of their friends had arranged. Some more strict than others, but overall the couple had never had a bad experience.

"Before we begin," Carlisle spoke up once all the people were accounted for. While Chelsey and Brandon's party was informal and reserved for a small handful of close friends and a lucky select few, Carlisle loved bringing new people into the fold, which meant that there were always formal introductions. He held a clipboard in front of him, from which he was going to be reading the rules, Liam knew. Not because he didn't know them, because everyone who frequented Carlisle's parties knew the rules by heart but because it gave off an official and serious air.

"The rules."

The people in attendance stood quietly and listened intently. A few hands went up to ask a question or to request clarification, and when Carlisle had run through the list, everyone consented to the rules.

"Now, as you can see, this room is pretty drab." Carlisle's comment elicited a few chuckles and elicited a scoff and a playful punch from his husband. It was a standard kitchen, designed in such a way that there was enough room for everyone to sit or stand comfortably. There was a sofa and a few bean bags for seating along with a few chairs around a fairly large coffee table upon which a canteen stood ready to dispense coffee.

As usual, there was not a drop of alcohol to be seen.

"This will be our neutral space for the evening. There will be no petting, no touching, no requests. You can come here to talk and wind down, but you will keep it strictly clean."

"If you are uncomfortable about anything at all, come find David or me," Carlisle indicated his husband by his side and added, "If you have a question, ask someone. We are always more than happy to guide you in the right direction." There were murmurs of agreement. "Follow me," Carlisle said as he swaggered through the kitchen door to his left.

Liam and Josie were hanging back to allow the group to pass first. That's when he saw her. Liam tugged on his wife's elbow and indicated to the short woman in front of them. Her dark hair was carefully braided down her back with what looked like a million tiny butterflies woven in. After a short tour of the rooms and another emphasis on consent and discussion, Carlisle led them to a large open-plan lounge that was wall-to-wall covered with shag carpeting. There were beanbags, pillows, and blankets everywhere. The lighting was dim and warm, creating a mood of instant comfort and homeliness.

"Kindly find a seat."
People whispered excitedly and plopped down wherever they were, eager to enjoy the planned festivities.

"There are a few new faces in the crowd and more than a few old friends." He grinned devilishly and added, "Let's get the awkward get-to-know-you drivel out of the way. I want each of you to stand and introduce yourself to the group, new and old."
It was pretty standard fare for Liam and Josie who stood up together to indicate that they are a pair - a sort of package deal - and introduced themselves. They were seen to be the resident "Mommy and Daddy" of the group and enjoyed the moniker. While not everyone in attendance followed the same line of enjoyment, there was not a single judgmental face in the crowd. People stood up at random as they felt the

courage to do so, and when the young woman with the glittery butterflies in her braided hair stood up, Liam and Josie paid close attention. She was dressed in a dark purple onesie underneath denim dungarees, "I'm Cammie." She nervously played with the end of her braid behind her back and licked her lips frequently.

"I'm 29, and I came here tonight too-" her voice shook, and her body was tense, "to make new friends and just be my little ol' self." Her face was beet red when she sat down, but the group cheered. Cammie hated the way her cheeks burned when she drew attention to herself.

Soon enough, everyone had been introduced. The group talked animatedly with each other, some turning around in their seats to look behind them, or leaning over others to greet.

"I want you to break up into small groups now."

What followed was a bonding experience and an exercise in voicing their choice to say 'no.' Carlisle guided them through how to say no, and especially how to remain firm if someone pressed the issue. He also covered and made the groups practice how to deal with another person's 'no.'

Liam had never really had trouble accepting no for an answer. He had learned early on that some people simply weren't interested, and he had learned to deal. Liam found their group's way of coping with being quite interesting. What struck him the most was the more simple of internal responses: "*I* am not what is being rejected, but my offer is."

Liam listened to each of Carlisle's hypothetical offers and descriptions of possible events with a slight amount of amusement. He had each of them reject the request. It ranged anywhere from "Can I touch your hands?" to "Can I watch while three of my friends fill your holes with their cocks."

It broke the ice, and everyone had a laugh. It emphasized that no matter what, a no is still a no.

When the games were over, Carlisle gave them

all a suggestive wink, "Have fun."

Those who wanted to stay and cuddle did so.
Other individuals and couples decided to move
to rooms more suited to their needs and desires.
One couple was whispering to one another,
touching each other's faces and hands. They
seemed to delight in doing nothing more than
simply being somewhere comfortable with each
other.

Cammie was tightly gripping the hand of another
Little, who was animatedly talking to her Daddy.
Liam recognized Ella, but it was the first time he
had seen her attend a party with someone. Liam
assumed it was simply because she enjoyed being
in her little space by herself rather than
accompanied by someone, but that was only a
guess. Cammie looked a little nervous, but after a
whisper from her friend, a smile broke, and she
eagerly followed behind Ella as she led her to the
corner. The pair started piling up pillows and
blankets to create a sort of pillow fort around the
small table in their corner.

Liam and Josie watched as a few other girls took

up another corner of the room and pulled
coloring books from their bags. One girl pointed
to a pack of crayons, "Can I borrow a crayon
from you?"

There was a short moment of hesitation, but the
girl consented and passed her the pack. The rest
of the exchanges were familiar to Liam. He felt
Josie's hand squeeze his. They were both
watching the girls as they went about their play.
They were laughing and showing off their
onesies, stuffies, and one girl even shared her
sippy cup with another. The scene was
heartwarming, and he felt a surge of
protectiveness rush through him. Josie squeezed
his hand again, and he knew she felt the same.
Hunter, the man that was with Ella and Cammie,
looked uncomfortably folded up as he was
squeezed into the small space next to Ella. He
whispered something to her, and she giggled so
hard she fell over. Her display made Cammie
grin, and Liam noticed her shoulders relax a
little. With a grunt and a flourish, Hunter
wriggled out from the tiny space before he was

set upon by Ella, who tickled him. He retaliated and ticked back, causing tears to roll down her cheeks from laughter.

"Be good, Ella. I'll be right back."

"Yes, Daddy!" Her eyes followed Hunter to where Liam and Josie were standing, arms wrapped around each other as they watched the display. Ella waved her greeting and returned to her pages, scooting closer to Cammie so that they could share.

He shook hands with both Liam and Josie, who commented on how natural he and Ella looked together.

His laugh was deep but bubbly, "I would hope so, she's my fiancé."

The surprise was evident. "Have you thought about collaring?" The words were out before Josie could stop herself, and Liam suppressed a smile.

Hunter laughed again, "Ella is perfectly capable of expressing her wants and needs. There's no need for a collar to keep unwanted attention away."

"What about Cammie? Is she yours, too?"

"Oh no, not at all. She's a close friend and decided to come with us instead of staying home."

Liam and Josie shared a meaningful glance that Hunter found amusing.

"Could you introduce us, you know, formally?" Josie asked a little too eagerly, and Liam squeezed her hand to help temper her excitement. He didn't want her to get her hopes up. There was no guarantee that Cammie would even accept the offer from them.

"She's captivating, isn't she?" Hunter looked over at Cammie, "She has that effect on people, and once they get to know her, *bam,* she's wormed her way into their hearts." He turned back to look at Liam and Josie, a knowing smile on his face.

"Have you ever had your own Little?"

"We have yet to find the perfect match," Liam admitted.

Without a word, Hunter returned to the table. He squatted down next to Ella and spoke softly to the two of them. Liam and Josie could hear nothing over the joyous laughter that came from the other table. The girls were now climbing over each other, tickling and blowing raspberries on any piece of exposed skin they could find. They had made a little game of trying to see who could elicit the most giggles.

There was a tense moment where Liam could feel his heart compress in his chest when Cammie looked at them. She looked so sweet and innocent, and it awoke a primal part of him that just wanted to hold her close and protect her from the world. He knew Josie felt the same way. It was part of why he loved her so much.

Cammie had agreed.

They felt as though their hearts would burst.

The group beckoned them over.

Cammie scooted up to make room for Josie, and Ella sat in Hunter's lap to allow a little room for Liam, who also seemed to be struggling to fit his tall frame into the small space.

"Can I see what you were drawing, Cammie?" Josie asked. The girl shook her head so vigorously that Josie feared butterflies were going to fly away.

"It's not ready yet," Cammie replied in a small voice.

"That's okay. Then can I draw something for you?" A smile broke open on her face. Liam hadn't noticed that Hunter and Ella had quietly disappeared until he moved to make himself a bit more comfortable.

"Can you draw a mouse?"

"A mouse?" Liam asked, leaning closer, "Why a mouse?"

"I like them. They're my favorite. So cute and small, and they have big ears!" Cammie's excitement grew as she talked. She told them of the pet mouse she had once had. She tried to draw it for them, too, but couldn't quite succeed. Liam and Josie saw her frustration.

"That's a pretty good mouse, Cammie." Liam offered. He handed her his picture that was also of a mouse, but all they could make out was the big ears and a long tail.
It elicited a small giggle from both Josie and

Cammie, but she still looked forlorn.

"I can teach you how to draw a mouse," Josie said as she slowly reached her hand across the table to Cammie. She let it rest there - an invitation.

Cammie wasn't sure what to think of Liam, or Josie, for that matter. They seemed kind enough, but again, so did her previous Daddy. It wasn't something she wanted to discuss - not here, not now.

But how could she explain to them that their kindness was actually hurting her?

Cammie abruptly got up, dropped the crayon she was holding, whispered a soft, "No, thank you." followed by an apology, and disappeared.

***

Cammie entered the kitchen, feeling a little lost, a little unsure of herself. While she hadn't had many expectations, she did hope to hit it off with *someone*. She felt stressed and was on the verge of tears.

"What do you need, honey?" David was at her side in an instant. He seemed to have an instinct for when people felt...out of their depth.

"Just a cup of coffee." Cammie's reply was curt, she realized, and added, "Pretty please. I'm dying for a fix."

David smiled, content with her request. Politeness was key.

"Do you have cream? Or whipped cream? I'll even take half-and-half if you have it." Cammie asked as she looked over the contents of the little fridge they were permitted to use. She stopped herself from asking for alcohol. It was a rule. No alcohol anywhere on the property, but she felt as though she needed it.

She had met a lovely couple: Liam and Josie. But to her, they seemed uninterested. They had talked and played and drawn pictures, but she wanted more. She wanted to cuddle but wasn't sure how to ask for it. She wanted them to take care of her. Liam and Josie. So she turned to the next best thing: whipped cream.

David set the can next to her, where she was

seated at the table, scooping a ton of sugar into her mug, "Want to talk about it?"

Cammie looked startled, and her face turned beet red again.

"Not a lot of people want whipped cream with their coffee. With other things, yes, but not with coffee. Especially not in these circles." David's eyes glittered, and a smile tugged at his lips, and his gaze softened, "I know an emotional soother when I see one, honey."

At that, he squirted a generous amount into her coffee and pulled a small shaker from the cupboard, "My secret stash."

"Chocolate sprinkles!" Cammie generously covered the cream in sprinkles and immediately dug in.

A soft chuckle came from the doorway. Josie hadn't meant to eavesdrop but was delighted to see Cammie so excited over something she thought mundane. Given her abrupt departure from their table, Josie was glad to see her smile at all.

"No, no, don't stop on my account," Josie

said as Cammie made to put the cup down. She suppressed another chuckle at Cammie's white mustache and poured herself a cup of coffee. Josie sat down across of Cammie. Close enough to feed her desire to take care of the woman but also far enough away as not to suffocate her.

"Listen," Josie said after an awkward moment of silence, "if we came on too strong, I'm sorry."

After another pause, Cammie broke the silence, "It's not that, Josie. I guess my expectations were a little skewed."

"What do you mean?"

"I-" Cammie paused, and a shadow passed over her features. She *really* needed a drink right now. "My life is a mess. I expected to find some way to escape that tonight. If anything, I think all I did was make an even bigger mess." Cammie scooped some cream with her finger and stuck it in her mouth. She could tell Josie was waiting for her to finish. Most people would blunder on and change the focus to themselves. Cammie appreciated it, then, with a deep sigh, added, "I

actually don't know what I was looking for."
Josie looked at the girl in front of her. They weren't that far apart in age, but Cammie really did give off this vulnerability that made Josie ache to hold her and promise her everything will be okay.

"That's the thing about messes, Cammie. You can always clean them up with the right help." Josie smiled reassuringly and handed Cammie a napkin for her whipped cream mustache, "Come find me if you want to talk." Josie disappeared through the doorway, and Cammie poked the cream with the tip of her finger and licked it off.
David was busying himself at the oven, pulling a fresh batch of cookies from its depths.

"David?" Cammie asked, "How well do you know Liam and Josie?"

"Honey, they are the fiercest, kindest, and most generous people I have ever had the pleasure to meet." David handed her a warm cookie and bit into one himself.

"But-" he said, between bites, "-you

should spend time with them to see for yourself. Different strokes." David savored another cookie and returned to the oven to bake the next batch. "It's okay if you don't hit it off with anyone. Don't feel pressured to have this be that moment for you. Sometimes it takes a couple of tries. Life's funny like that."

"Thank you for the coffee, David," Cammie said, and her heartfelt a little lighter as she took a bite of her cookie.

***

The one-on-one diaper playroom was fully stocked along with a side table filled with lotions, creams, and powders. A single bed was pushed up against the wall, right next to the changing table.

There was a second, larger bed opposite the first, that could accommodate snuggles, cuddles, and possibly other forms of play if there was consent. Liam and Josie knew that there would be nothing more than caregiving today. It was what the three of them had agreed to. Cammie didn't want anything more, and truth be told, neither did Josie or Liam.

It was not a private room by any means, but it did preclude anyone from joining unless they had permission from all parties present. Cammie stood just inside the doorway, a red blush creeping up her neck again. Josie noticed, "What's the matter, little one?"

Her voice was so low that Josie had to put her ear right up to Cammie's lips to hear, "I had an accident." Cammie's voice was breaking. Josie held her close and hushed her.

"There's nothing to be ashamed about, little mouse." Liam's soothing voice caused her to look up at him with wide, trusting eyes, tears brimming them.

"Let's get you cleaned up. Then we can do something together."

"Can we read a story?"

"Whatever you want, little one," Josie said, kissing Cammie's flushed cheek as she guided her to the changing station. Cammie's face lit up, momentarily forgetting her wet diaper.

Cammie unclipped the dungaree straps with a little difficulty, but she had insisted on doing that herself, and she let the overalls crumple to a heap at her feet. Liam had laid out a soft, clean sheet over the bed.

"Good job, little one." Josie helped Cammie get up on the single bed and instructed her to lie on her back. Josie carefully spread her legs apart and reached between them to unclip the onesie. Liam had started pulling out cream and baby powder and setting them on the end table within Josie's reach.

She pushed the hem of the onesie over Cammie's soft, warm skin, delighting in the goosebumps that were spreading from her touch. The diaper crinkled as Cammie squirmed and giggled, "That tickles, Mommy."

Josie chuckled, her smile was contagious, "Hold still, please."

Cammie stuck her thumb in her mouth and watched both Liam and Josie as the first fastening was removed with a rough tearing noise, then the other. Josie carefully pulled the front of the diaper down. Her breath caught in her throat. Cammie's pussy lips were shaved clean. There was not a hair or blemish in sight, except for one, tiny beauty mark.

Getting her voice back, Josie instructed Cammie to lift her hips so that they could remove the diaper completely. Cammie did as she was told, dutifully lifting her hips, providing Josie with a delicious view.

"Look at that! Not such a big mess, little girl. You're doing well." Josie exclaimed and handed the wet diaper off to Liam, who carefully folded it closed and discarded it into the bin. Josie grabbed a wet wipe and started to clean Cammie off. She started with the inner thigh where some urine had been smeared. Josie moved the wipe in circles, first the one leg, then the other. Cammie spread her legs, her face flushed with something other than shame this time. "Don't forget the most important part, Mommy."

Liam's cock jerked. Her gesture wasn't as innocent as the rest of their play, but he stilled the urge to touch her.

Josie used a clean wipe and started on her lips. The cloth was so thin that it may as well not have been there. Her fingers ran over the swollen nub, and Cammie moaned softly. Her own core burned in response. Josie continued cleaning her baby girl up, making sure to wipe down every spot.

Liam handed Josie the bottle of baby cream.

"What's that for, Mommy?" Cammie asked.

"It's cream so that the diaper doesn't give your soft bottom a rash," Josie said.

Josie massaged the cream into Cammie's soft ass and over her mound, careful not to let her fingers linger too long.

Liam handed her a fresh diaper. Again, Cammie lifted her hips. Josie set the diaper in place, and Cammie dropped her hips, her thumb still in her mouth and her big eyes watching them.

Josie sprinkled some baby powder into the

palms of her hands and ran them over her skin. The scent was fresh and lovely. It reminded her of home. Cammie felt at ease. They were polite and followed her wishes, even if her little body had betrayed her when Josie touched her.

The diaper was fastened, and she was told to get up. Carefully, the fabric of the onesie was rolled down and refastened.

"Do you want to put your dungarees back on?"

Cammie shook her head.

"Use your words, little mouse," Liam said.

"No, Mommy."

"Then, I think you should hang it up over the chair so that it doesn't wrinkle." Josie helped Cammie shake it out and fold it carefully over the armrest of the only chair in the room.

"Good job, Cammie."

Liam got comfortable on the bed and patted the spot next to him. Cammie looked expectantly at Josie, who nodded and patted her bottom, "You go snuggle, and I'll pick out a book for us to read."

Cammie squealed with joy and launched herself into Liam's arms. A tickle war ensued, and Liam's rich laughter mixed in with Cammie's sweet voice made Josie's heart swell. This is what she wanted, and it was amazing.

"Alright you two, what do you want to read?" Josie asked and made herself comfortable on Cammie's other side as her fits of laughter slowly quieted.

"What are our choices?" Liam asked, reaching out to tuck a strand of Josie's hair. He felt at home.

"Well, there is Little Red Riding Hood," Josie suggested, "Daddy can make all the noises for the Big Bad Wolf. He's amazing."

"Oh, no, that sounds too scary!" Cammie commented and pulled her stockinged legs up. Liam wrapped his arms around her and kissed the top of her head, "It's okay, little mouse, it's just a story."

"Or how about a story just for you?" Josie ventured, "The Tales of Despereaux. It's about a little mouse who acts too different from other mice, so they try to teach him to stop being different."

"Were they mean to him, Mommy?" Josie smiled, "Let's find out together."

They sat snuggled together on the bed, Cammie listening intently. She gasped in the right places, laughed when the little mouse did something funny, and was scared when he was in danger. Liam had made the voices for the bad guys, deepening it to almost a growl. He made his voice light and squeaky for the little mouse. He also made the noises of the pots bubbling in the kitchen, or the sound of a mouse chewing on paper.

Cammie was enthralled. Liam and Josie were caring and kind. They let her ask questions. They held her. And they played with her. They demanded nothing.

Chapter 3

On a rare weekend off together, Liam and Josie lay in each other's arms, the curtains drawn against the mid-morning sunlight.

"I have a surprise for you," Liam whispered as he kissed her neck and collarbone, eliciting a sigh of content from Josie.

"But that means we have to get up," he said as he immediately rolled out of bed, and Josie protested.

"I was comfortable." Josie huffed and sat up, hair messed, and her lips swollen. Liam pulled in to kiss her, "It'll be fun, I promise."

***

Liam's first stop, and to Josie's surprise, was a little lingerie shop.

"I'm here to collect my order," Liam said, his arms still around his wife, holding her close to him. The staff looked on in envy. Josie could tell by the way their eyes glossed over that they were imagining Liam doing all kinds of things to them.

A faint blush crept onto her cheek when she noticed a few of those salacious looks were aimed at her. The attention had started a warm tingle in the center of her body that steadily grew warmer and started to pulse as Liam unperturbed ran his hand down her body.

"Mr. Everhart, your order." The saleswoman carefully placed the package in front of him and unfolded the tissue paper that was wrapped around it. Liam stepped close, removed the garment from the parcel, and held it up for Josie to inspect.

A black, snakeskin patterned lace outfit with leather ties, garter straps, and an adjustable choker. When Josie stroked the fabric, it was much softer than it appeared. Smooth and almost as soft as silk.

"It's gorgeous, Liam." Josie breathed.

"Would the lady like to be fitted for the

garment?" The question seemed innocent enough, but neither Josie nor Liam missed the lustful undertone at the suggestion of the saleswoman.

A twinkle in her eye told Liam that Josie was more than willing.

Liam waited outside the dressing room as Josie changed into her gift. Josie stripped naked and looked at her sleek, defined form in the mirror. As she slid into the garment, the soft lace and cool leather contrasted one another, caressing her skin and causing goosebumps to spread across her body.

Josie admired her reflection. Liam knew exactly what she wanted. The corset hugged her body, accentuating her curves. The adjustable leather straps that ran between her breasts were tantalizing. Josie pulled on the stockings that came with the garment and clipped them to the garter straps. It fit like a glove.

Josie emerged from the dressing room with a flourish, grinning broadly at the breathless expressions on the faces of her audience.

Cammie, tucked into the corner and trying to keep her head down, turned to look at the commotion. Her heart jumped into her throat, and she blinked a couple of times to make sure that she wasn't hallucinating.

"Josie," she whispered, and an immediate heat flooded through her. There was no denying that the woman was built like a goddess. Cammie's feet guided her, unbidden, closer...closer...close enough that she could almost reach out and touch Josie.

Their eyes met, and a spark ignited deep inside of her. The garment only alluded to the forbidden places on the woman's body, but Cammie's desire built regardless. She shuffled, becoming a little uncomfortable but kept her eyes locked on Josie's.

Cammie was still holding her bralette and panties, she realized, as Josie closed the gap between them. Liam also only noticed Cammie now, and a warm smile crinkled his eyes, "Cammie, what a pleasant surprise."

Her return greeting was a little half-hearted, but

Liam knew the reason behind it. Josie's walk was dominating, her hips swaying seductively. Josie's gaze drifted to the garments Cammie was clutching, and a blush crept up her neck. It was a simple style, but still cute. Pink ribbons adorned the straps of the bralette and the front of the panties.

***

"Here," Josie said and handed a stack of clothes to Cammie. Instinctively, Cammie took them but stuttered out an apology, "J-Josie, I appreciate you helping me choose something, but I really can't afford any of this."

Not a complete lie. Cammie had *some* funds in her account but had been planning on spending the evening at a bar. Something to take her mind off of her job, her life, and her unsatisfied sex life. Hopefully, getting buzzed just enough that she wouldn't mind going home with a complete stranger.

When Cammie hesitated, Josie placed a gentle

hand on hers, "You don't have to get anything you want to, Cammie. It's for completely selfish reasons," Josie said. "I want to see what they would look like on you."

Cammie smiled, a little turned on at the thought of Josie seeing her completely naked. With a small nod, Cammie agreed and headed to the changing room, Josie, in tow.

***

Cammie had really started to relax around Liam and Josie. She watched how the two interacted with each other and with others. She had taken David's advice and had taken the chance to get to know them.

They both intimidated her, but she doubted it was purposeful. Whenever Josie noticed that Cammie was feeling uncomfortable, she had gone out of her way to set Cammie at ease. Josie had joked about the pink bralette and panties, but it was lighthearted and fun. After seeing how confident Josie was and how unsuggestive any of her comments or questions were, Cammie had felt silly for being ashamed about buying such sexy undergarments.

As the day wore on, the pair had invited Cammie along to lunch, and eventually, they made their way to a nearby park where they could enjoy the rest of the beautiful day.

Just as Josie had made Cammie feel at ease, Liam had done the same. Liam would subtly change topics or phrase questions in such a way that Cammie didn't feel forced to answer, but rather that she had *wanted* to answer them. Liam had asked her about her job. Her parents, her friends, and soon enough, the sun was starting to set.

"How long have the two of you..." Cammie trailed off.

"Been Caregivers?" Liam said, finishing Cammie's question.

"Yes," Cammie replied, looking down at her feet.

There was a small pause before Liam answered, "A year or so into our marriage, we started talking about fantasies. We met some people, made some friends, and went to our first play party."

"That was about five years ago," Josie added.

"How many Littles do you take care of?"

"We stand in as we need to, but we have never officially adopted a Little of our own."

"Would you want to?" Cammie asked, but hastily added, "I mean, the other Littles seem to flock around the two of you, and you seem happy. I just mean-"
Josie laughed, "We understand what you mean, Cammie."

"We *are* happy, little mouse. We have grown to love them, even if they have their own full-time Daddies or Mommies," Liam said.

"We want to, but it's not always possible," Josie added.

"Would you-" Cammie pursed her lips, her heart was hammering in her chest so hard she was sure than Liam and Josie could hear it, "would you want me?"

The split second of time that followed the request was the longest of her life, but Cammie kept a brave face and braced for the worst.

"Cammie, sweetheart, we would love nothing more," Liam whispered.

Liam and Josie felt as though they had struck gold. This sweet, shy girl wanted them. Both of them, as they were.

Tears were threatening to fall, and Cammie looked away. It was tenuous, but hope bloomed in her chest as she whispered, "Promise? You're not just making fun of me?"

"We would never make fun of you, Cammie," Josie said, holding her hand out to Cammie. She scooted closer and hugged Josie, listening to her heartbeat and feeling the warmth of her body through the dress.

"It's getting late," Josie said.

"Cammie, would you like to come home with us?" Liam asked.

Cammie pulled away from Josie to stare at them. Liam was smiling reassuringly. "It would be no imposition, Cammie," he added.

"We would like to have your company if you'd do us the honor," Josie said, patting her hand.

Josie's next words weren't quite as innocent. This time Cammie knew the question held more than the prospect of simply visiting them for dinner. Perhaps it was the way it was phrased, or by the way, Josie's gaze darkened as she looked at her, but Cammie could see her attraction clear as day. "You can stay over if you'd like."

***

Cammie was in awe. The house was the most beautiful place she had ever seen. It was breathtaking. Magnificent. Cammie ran out of words to use to describe it. It wasn't enormous, but it was imposing in its sleek architecture.

"The house has been in my family for years," Liam said. The stunned look on Cammie's face filled him with pride. "You two go inside while I grab our things."

Cammie followed behind Josie as she let herself

in. The house was more beautiful inside than it was out, and Cammie gawked.

"Come now, little one, let's show you around." Josie hooked her arm through Cammie's, and off they went. By the time they had worked their way through the house, both upstairs and the cozy little yard outside, Liam had brought in all their shopping bags and had poured them each something to drink, making himself comfortable on the leather couch in the living room.

"I have something I think you would like, little one," Josie said as Cammie made herself comfortable next to Liam on the couch. Curiosity got the better of her, and Cammie hopped to her feet. Josie handed Cammie a small gift-wrapped package, "I saw how much you liked."

Cammie tore it open, her eyes watering a little, "I can keep it?"

"Yes, little one. It's all yours." Josie said. Cammie jumped excitedly and hugged her gift to her chest. It was the pink dress that she had fallen in love with at the store. It was covered in yellow bows and frills of white and gray. She threw her arms around Josie, pressing herself against her body, saying 'thank you' over and over again.

The longer she was pressed against Josie, the more aware she became of her body. What Cammie had seen in the store was now highlighted and enhanced by touch. Cammie could feel the heat of her skin against hers; she could smell Josie's scent.

Cammie felt the urge to kiss her. And then she did.

It was just a light peck. To say, thank you. But then Cammie kissed her again, and this time she let her lips linger. Cammie savored the feel of feminine lips against hers, so soft and demanding at the same time. Josie's arms tightened, and she kissed Cammie back, losing herself in that single moment.

Josie's tongue searched out hers. Cammie broke the kiss by stepping back, her face flushed, and her breathing a little uneven.

"Can I go try it on, Mommy?" Cammie asked.

"Of course you can, Cammie," Josie said and licked her lips, "but show Daddy the dress after you've put it on. He hasn't seen it yet." Cammie dashed into the nearest room and changed, stripping her tight jeans and crop top off. She had stripped completely naked, enjoying the freedom. She pulled the dress over her head and smiled as she ran her fingertips over the little gray mouse embroidered over her heart. Cammie's lips still tingled where they had touched Josie's, and she let her hand roam, touching herself.

The excitement of what was to come was slowly building up within her, and Cammie stroked herself, loving the sensation.

Cammie ran back to where Liam and Josie were sitting in the lounge and interrupted their talk with her outburst, "Look how pretty my new dress is, Daddy!"

Cammie threw herself onto the couch and locked her arms around them, nuzzling their faces excitedly.

"Little mouse," Liam's voice was firm, and his look sucked away just a little of the excitement as he carefully pulled her away from him.

"Yes, Daddy?" Cammie asked, embarrassment flooding her.

"Good little girls don't interrupt people when they're talking, do they?"

"No, Daddy."

"Are you a good girl, Cammie?"

"Yes, Daddy. I'm sorry, Daddy. I just got all excited."

Liam chuckled and stroked her arm to let her know he wasn't angry, "Good, now what is it you wanted to show us?"

Cammie got up off of the couch and twirled; the little ribbons and frills dancing as she moved. "See, I look almost like a princess," Cammie whispered gleefully as she twirled again.

"Oh, but you *are* a princess, Cammie." Josie beamed.

"Only a real princess could look as

beautiful as you," Liam cooed and motioned for Cammie to come a little closer.

"Can I sit on your lap, Daddy?" Cammie asked, holding the folds of her dress in her fists and swishing the skirt around playfully.

"Yes, little mouse."

Cammie carefully sat herself down in Liam's lap. She could feel his hardness pressed against her thigh, and it caused a jolt of pleasure to shoot through her.

"Am I hurting you, Daddy?"

"Not at all, sweetheart." Liam's voice was thick. Not a lie, but his cock was straining against the zipper of his jeans, which was beginning to sit uncomfortably.

Cammie wrapped her arms around Liam's neck and pressed her face into his shoulder. She felt comfortable, warm, and perfectly safe.

Cammie, feeling a little naughty, pulled away from Liam, looked him dead in the eye, and licked his cheek. Taking advantage of the brief moment of surprise, Cammie disengaged and darted away, giggling hysterically.

Josie laughed and watched as Liam set off after her. The laughter echoing in the house was a beautiful sound.

"Be careful you two," She called, still smiling broadly. Cammie whipped past her, her skirt lifting up high behind her as she jumped over the furniture. After a few more minutes, Liam and Cammie fell to the carpet at Josie's feet out of breath.

"Join us, Mommy!"

Liam held his hand out to her, and Josie slid onto the floor. Their lips met, and fire burned between them.

Liam felt Cammie fiddle with the buckle on his belt. She was biting her bottom lip and rubbing his cock through the fabric of his jeans.

"Mommy, can you help me, please?"

Josie showed Cammie how to undo Liam's belt with one hand, and the girl beamed, "I did it!"

"You're a smart girl, little mouse," Liam whispered, his voice husky and deep.

Josie instructed Cammie how to undo the buttons on the jeans, and together, they freed his throbbing cock. Cammie immediately wrapped her warm hands around it and began squeezing softly. He grabbed a handful of hair and guided Cammie's lips to the head of his cock.

Josie got on her knees and demonstrated, "Carefully, like this."

Cammie watched as Josie's expert hands stroked Liam's cock, and her tongue flicked over the head, causing his cock to twitch uncontrollably.

"Slow," he commanded.

Josie grinned broadly at Cammie, a naughty twinkle in her eye, "You try, baby girl."

Cammie felt moisture pool between her legs. She had decided to go commando under the dress and felt daring for doing so. Her heart raced, exhilarated. Cammie copied Josie's movements almost exactly, first stroking him with her hands, then flicking her tongue over and around the head of his swollen member. It twitched, and a bead of liquid formed at the tip.

Then, locking eyes with Liam, she opened her mouth and sucked the head of his cock into it, flicking her tongue over the sensitive tip.

"Good girl," Josie said as she ran her hands over Cammie's thighs, feeling her quake. Her own body was screaming for release, but she wanted to make sure Cammie knew how to please her Daddy properly.

"Slowly, and be careful not to hurt Daddy with your teeth, little girl."

Cammie continued stroking Liam's thick cock with her hands and mouth, enjoying the taste of him. She suckled on the head of his cock and delighted it the blissed-out look on Liam's face. Josie gently pulled Cammie away and pressed her lips to Cammie's. She tasted faintly of Liam and sugar. Josie kissed her harder, running her hand down Cammie's small body, tasting her with her tongue.

Josie broke off the kiss and tucked a strand of hair behind Cammie's ear.

"Watch me carefully, little one."

She showed Cammie how to take all of Liam's thick cock into her mouth and into her throat. Cammie watched as Liam's eyes' rolled to the back of his head just as Josie's tongue caressed the underside of his balls. Josie continued sucking Liam's cock, pulling away until just his tip remained in her mouth, then expertly swallowing his cock until the whole thing was no longer visible to Cammie.

Liam groaned his pleasure.

"Can I try, Mommy?" Cammie asked, edging closer, feeling moisture coat her inner thighs.

"Not yet, little mouse," Liam said and sat up as Josie finally released him. His cock jerked wildly as he suppressed the urge to cum.

"Why not, Daddy?" Cammie asked, not bothering to hide the hurt, "Did I do something wrong?"

"You did wonderfully, Cammie," Liam said thickly, "but I want you to help Mommy undress while I catch my breath."

Cammie's eyes glittered as she understood, and Josie helped her to her feet. Josie turned around and pulled her hair out of the way to give Cammie access to the zipper of her dress. Cammie, driven by the super-charged sexual tension between them, unzipped the dress slowly, making sure to let her fingers caress her skin as they trailed down her back. Electricity passed between them.

Josie stepped out of the dress and stood to face Cammie and Liam. Her undergarments were simple, not at all like the gift Liam had gotten her earlier that day. Her hands caressed Josie's breasts, testing their weight, and her fingers slipped under the wired support, stroking the bare skin of her breasts. Cammie's fingers found the front clasp.

Cammie licked her lips.

"Keep going, little mouse, you're doing so well." Her body throbbed with need at Liam's words; his cock still out and rock hard, precum glistening on the head. Cammie gently grabbed the elastic of Josie's thong and slid her hands down her outer thighs. Cammie's face was now perfectly aligned with Josie's swollen lips, and she could see moisture glistening between their folds. Josie's scent was intoxicating, and without asking, Cammie leaned forward and flicked her tongue over Josie's slit, tasting the dew that glittered there.

"Stop," Josie said.

"Why?" Cammie couldn't suppress her whine of frustration and sat back on her heels, looking up at Josie with a mix of irritation and desperation. She wanted to taste all of Josie, and she wanted to feel Liam's cock pushing inside of her. Cammie wanted both of them to hold her while she pleasured them and they pleasured her.

"Girls who don't listen to their Mommies get punished." Liam's voice sent another jolt of heat through her as he wrapped his arms around Josie from behind and slid his fingers into her wet pussy, letting it coat his fingers.

"It's not fair, Daddy!"

"Cammie." A warning clear in Liam's voice.

"But Daddy."

"Stand up, little mouse," Liam commanded, still playing with his wife's pussy. Cammie stood, pouting. It was a bad move, and she knew it, but Cammie wasn't going to be denied.

"Go to the room and wait for me." Liam's voice held the promise of a good spanking, and Cammie could already feel her bottom sting. Cammie folded her arms and huffed.

"Don't make Daddy repeat himself, Cammie." Josie's voice imitated Liam's in its seriousness.

"No." Her words were barely cold when Liam pulled his belt free from his jeans. Cammie gulped and involuntarily took a step back.

"Bend over, now."

Cammie shivered. She heard the steel in his voice but also felt the sexual tension climb.

"Daddy."

Liam closed the distance between them and gently, and with practiced movement, spun Cammie around, and bent her over the armrest of the couch. He lifted the skirt of the dress over her ass and paused.

"No panties?" Liam asked, unable to hide his surprise. Cammie could feel his cock press against her bare ass cheek, and she swallowed in anticipation.

"No, Daddy."

Liam stroked Cammie's bare ass, the skin was soft, and her cheeks were firm. Liam pulled back a little to allow room for what came next, "Count."

"Daddy, no, I-"

Whack.

Her ass stung, and the sound was ringing in her ears.

"One."

Whack.

"Two."

Cammie squeezed her eyes shut as Liam spanked her with his belt. It wasn't hard enough to leave a mark, but it was hard enough to make his point. When she reached ten, he set the belt down and gently rubbed her now red cheeks. He spread them apart, letting his fingers touch her pussy lips. Cammie quivered.

"It looks like our little girl enjoyed that, Josie."

Josie took Liam's place behind Cammie. Cammie was trembling and panting, "I'm sorry, Daddy." Josie's tongue surprised Cammie as she pushed it between her pussy lips, flicking her swollen clit. She gasped and moaned out loud. Josie inserted first one finger, then two into her dripping pussy.

"Are you going to behave now, baby girl?" Josie whispered as she kissed the soft skin of her ass, letting her fingers slide in and out of Cammie's pussy.

"Yes, Mommy." With that, Josie sped up her strokes, and Cammie came hard. Her body twitched, and she screamed out loud, "Fuck!" Liam thrust his cock into her spasming pussy, and Cammie swore again. He pulled out and, panting, Cammie tried to push back onto his cock, "I'm sorry, Daddy, don't stop."

"What do we say?" Liam used the flat of his hand and spanked her.

"Please, Daddy, please put it back in." Liam pushed in slowly as he rubbed her raw ass cheek. He spanked her again as he pulled out.

"Daddy." Cammie was pleading with him. Her moans grew louder with each firm *whack* and soon orgasmed a second time, her pussy clamping down on his cock, and she writhed beneath him.

Josie crawled onto the couch and kissed Cammie, drawing more moans from her. Josie positioned herself and spread her legs, presenting her own swollen and wet pussy to Cammie, "Please lick Mommy's pussy, little girl." Cammie licked her lips and obeyed, her body still twitching, and her mind foggy.

Josie threw her head back and moaned, grabbing a fistful of hair, she kept Cammie's lips pressed to her pussy lips, feeling her sweet, warm tongue flick and probe, drawing pleasure from her.

"That's right, little one, just like that." Liam encouraged Cammie. The look of ecstasy on his wife's face and the tight pussy stroking his cock brought him dangerously close to an orgasm. Liam slowed his strokes, and with his thumb, he circled Cammie's ass hole, coating it in her own juices. She moaned as he slowly

pushed a finger into her tight hole, her body
tensing.

"Relax your muscles, little mouse."
Cammie obeyed, and he started a slow rhythm,
matching his thrusts into her pussy.
It was a new and strange sensation, but it
heightened her arousal, making her body twitch
again, "Oh, Daddy."
Liam grunted and pulled his cock out of
Cammie's pussy. After working her ass for a few
more minutes, Cammie's moans were nearly as
loud as his wife's. Josie had her head thrown
back, her fingers pinching and pulling her own
nipples as Cammie's fingers worked their way in
and out of her wetness.
Liam pressed the head of his thick member
against Cammie's lubricated ass hole. Cammie
gasped and pushed back slightly.

"Daddy, put your cock in my ass and make
me cum again," Cammie cried out as he pushed
inside of her. His cock stretching her ass hole,
filling her to the brim.
Josie orgasmed loudly, bucking against

Cammie's fingers, her face flushed from pleasure. She saw the look of concentration on Liam's face as he attempted to keep himself in check.

"Tell Daddy what you want, Cammie," Josie whispered, running her thumb over Cammie's bottom lip. Josie wanted to see the look on Liam's face as he filled their little girl with his hot cum.

"Fuck me hard, Daddy," Cammie said breathlessly as she waited for him to thrust into her tight hole. Her body had adjusted to his size and relaxed accordingly. Her pussy twitched in anticipation as Liam massaged her ass cheeks, then gripped her hips, holding her in place.

"Please, Daddy?" Cammie begged. Liam lost control as his baby girl begged for his cock. He spread her ass cheeks apart and started pumping his cock in and out of Cammie's ass. Cammie pushed back onto his cock and moaned loudly. Her voice caused his cock to throb and twitch as he fucked her.

"Make me cum, Daddy." Cammie could

feel her body on edge. It was a different feeling, more intense. Cammie's body exploded as she orgasmed violently. Her eyes rolled to the back of her head as she screamed.

Liam thrust himself deep into Cammie's ass hole. Her orgasm was causing the muscles in her body to clench and tighten around him. Liam came instantly. His cock spurted cum deep into her ass. He threw his head back and clenched his teeth, groaning loudly as his orgasm ripped through him.

Spent, Liam pulled his cock free and joined the girls on the floor.

They lay intertwined on the soft plush carpet of the living room, panting. Cammie could feel her body still twitching from her previous orgasms. Her brain was fuzzy, and her limbs weak.

Josie was planting soft kisses over her eyes and face. Every part of her skin was sensitive to touch, and Cammie moaned in response as Josie drew her nails across the skin on Cammie's inner thighs.

Liam wrapped his arms around Cammie and

pulled her close to him, burying his nose in her hair. She smelled of a woman, sex, and flowers. His cock jerked, and he pressed it against Cammie's ass, making her moan again.

***

When they finally caught their breath after another round of play, it was well close to midnight.

"Let's get you cleaned up, little girl," Josie whispered as she moved to stand. Her legs were trembling, but her footing was steady. She held her hand out to Cammie, who took it, still dazed. The girl had a glow about her that Josie knew all too well. Liam was adept at drawing even the most reluctant of orgasms from anyone. Together the two women made their way to the bathroom. Josie added some bubble bath to the stream and watched as the warm water flowed into the tub, and steam started to fill the air. Josie helped Cammie into the tub and watched as she sighed and sank further down into the water. She allowed her to sit in silence for as long as she needed. Cammie felt the heaviness of her eyes and yawned, "Mommy, I'm sleepy."

"You need to wash yourself first, little Cammie. Then we can snuggle in bed together, okay?"

"Okay, Mommy." Cammie's movements were sluggish, and she dropped the bottle of body wash with a messy splash. Cammie giggled tiredly, "Please help me, Mommy."
Josie helped her lather and wash every inch of her body.

"I'm done now, Mommy," Cammie said proudly after she rinsed the soap from her skin all by herself.

"Good girl. Time to get out."
Cammie stood carefully and held her arms out. Josie wrapped her in a large, fluffy towel.

"Thank you, Mommy."
Josie guided Cammie to the kitchen and sat her down in the chair and kissed her forehead, "Daddy will make you a bottle, little one."

"Wait! Where are you going, Mommy?"

Cammie asked sleepily, trying to wriggle the chair around in order to see Josie.

"Mommy's going to go take a shower, Cammie," Liam said, drawing her attention back to him. While Cammie had been in the bath, Liam had taken a shower of his own. He smelled fresh and wore soft, silky-looking sweatpants, and Cammie could make out the length of his cock as the material caressed it.

"Okay, Daddy." Cammie was still wrapped in the warm embrace of the towel and was slowly starting to fall asleep in her seat. Liam chuckled, "Come, little mouse, here's your bottle." Liam handed her a baby bottle that was filled with a creamy looking liquid. The girl hadn't eaten since their early lunch, and he was sure she was famished. It was close to two in the morning, and he could feel his own stomach grumble unhappily. He had mixed up a serving of a good quality meal replacer for her and added an extra bit of vanilla syrup to sweeten it up. Cammie had shown to have a pretty big sweet tooth, both at lunch and during the last play party they had attended.

"What flavor did you make it, Daddy?" Cammie asked at the same time she popped the nipple in her mouth.

"Vanilla ice cream." Cammie smiled happily and continued drinking, her eyes drooping a little more, "Daddy, can we go to bed now?"

"Of course we can, little mouse, as soon as we get you dressed." Liam scooped her up easily enough and carried her to the spare bedroom where their toys were kept. Cammie was too sleepy to notice her surroundings, except how soft and inviting the bed felt beneath her. Cammie sighed happily as she sucked on the bottle, enjoying the creamy vanilla taste. It was thicker than a milkshake and just as sweet. Liam had brought some of Cammie's things in from the living room. He pulled a diaper from one of the bags and set it down on the end table. Liam gently pulled Cammie into a seated position, and the towel slipped from her shoulders.

"Stand for Daddy, please."

Cammie obeyed and was unsteady on her feet. Liam removed the towel and made her lie down again. Liam gripped Cammie by the ankles and lifted her legs and ass into the air as he swiftly slid the diaper underneath her.

Cammie giggled, "You're strong, Daddy."

Liam fastened the velcro straps of the diaper and turned to another of Cammie's bags. He had spied an onesie in there earlier and looked for it now. When he turned back, Cammie had the strangest look on her face. It took him a second to figure it out, and then Cammie giggled, "Sorry, Daddy."

She had wet herself.

Just then, Josie came into the room, saw the guilt on Cammie's face, the slight annoyance on Liam's, and chuckled, "What did you do, little one?"

"I had an accident," Cammie whispered, and her cheeks turning bright pink. She put the bottle back in her mouth and continued drinking.

Liam shook his head and smiled, "Our baby forgot to use the little girl's room before getting ready for bed."

"I'll grab a clean one," Josie said. Again, Liam gripped Cammie by the ankles, "Ready?" She nodded, and he hoisted her up, causing the girl to giggle. He pulled the wet diaper free, and Josie replaced it with a fresh one. She wiped Cammie down with a couple of baby wipes and then patted her bottom dry with the towel.

"I'm sorry, Daddy, I didn't mean to make a mess," Cammie whispered.

"It's okay, little mouse, accidents happen." Liam gently stroked her hair as Josie continued to fix the diaper.

When she was done, Josie helped Cammie into her new onesie, clipped it closed, and handed her over to Liam. Cammie had finished her bottle by now but was still suckling on the nipple, her eyes closed. Liam lifted Cammie and held her to him, her head resting on his shoulders.

Josie cleaned up and followed behind Liam as

the pair made their way to the main bedroom. Liam carefully lay Cammie down on the bed, and she squirmed to get comfortable, still sucking on the empty bottle.

"Here you go, sweetheart," Josie said, and removed the bottle, replacing it with Cammie's brand new paci. Without opening her eyes, Cammie adjusted it and continued suckling, a smile on her face.

Josie smiled at her sleeping form, "Our little girl is wonderful, Liam."

Liam and Josie, tired, but happy, crawled into bed with their little girl. Josie snuggled up to Cammie and wrapped her arms around her. Cammie mumbled something in her sleep and snuggled deeper into Josie's embrace.

Liam had gotten into bed on Cammie's other side and watched as his girls slept. He stroked Cammie's hair, content.

****

Early the next morning, Cammie had snuck out

of bed and went to grab a shower before work. Cammie was busy making coffee when Liam and Josie emerged from the room, completely dressed.

"Don't worry about your car," Josie said. "I've already made a call to have it safely transported to where you need it. All I need is an address."

"Don't look so panicked, little mouse," Liam said with a soft smile, giving her a quick hug before grabbing a cup of coffee. "I can drive you to work. We did invite you here after all." Cammie breathed a sigh of relief and gave the location to Josie. It was a little strange to watch the two of them act so completely normal after the fantastic night they had exploring each other's bodies.

Cammie had woken with Josie's protective arms still wrapped around her.

"Thank you for taking care of me," Cammie said shyly.

Josie kissed Cammie's forehead in a very maternal manner, and Cammie inhaled the scent of her skin and soap, "You're always welcome here, little one."

They exchanged numbers before Cammie dragged Liam out the door, "Quickly, Daddy, I'm going to be late."

Chapter 4

Come over this weekend, little mouse. We have another surprise for you.

Cammie bit her lip as she stared down at her phone, reading the message from Liam a few times before attempting a reply, typing and retyping. They had spent every day for the last few days messaging back and forth. They had set a few ground rules for her, and in turn, she had told them what she would and would not do. They had agreed, and so their friendship grew. *I'd love to, Daddy, but I can't. My friends are in town, and we're going out.* Fingers trembling, she hastily added, *I promised them I would be there.*

Cammie was a nervous wreck. She didn't want Liam or Josie to be disappointed, especially not this early on in their relationship. They had just gotten to know each other, and she really liked them. Something of a feat these days.

Are you telling me or asking me, Cammie?

Her heart hammering, she quickly typed her reply just as her Manager came into the back office and looked at her reproachfully.

Please, can I go, Daddy? I can't break my promise. Pretty please?

Cammie hadn't had a chance to check her messages again until the end of her shift but was relieved to see that Liam had agreed to her going out after all.

Thank you, Daddy! Cammie added a heart and a smiley face as an added cuteness. It was late Friday night, and Cammie had planned to have a couple of drinks with her colleagues but thought better of it and drove herself home.

Cammie dropped her keys and her bag on the kitchen counter and headed straight for the fridge. She pulled out the day-old Chow Mein and threw it into the microwave. As her food heated up, Cammie looked longingly at the open bottle of wine on the counter. Josie had strictly disapproved of Cammie drinking any alcohol while they spent time together, and as she thought about pouring herself a small glass to help her wind down, a bubble of disapproval tickled in the pit of Cammie's stomach.

Cammie shrugged off the feeling of guilt and poured the rest of the bottle into a large wine glass. *Better to finish it and remove future temptation*, she thought. Cammie ate her leftovers in silence. She missed the closeness she had shared with Liam and Josie.

Another thought occurred to her as she threw back the last of the wine. She wouldn't really be able to message Liam or Josie while her friends were in town. She toyed with the idea of simply switching her phone off and dealing with the aftermath later but thought better of it. Feeling slightly buzzed, Cammie shot Liam a quick message:

I won't be able to message a lot while I'm with my friends, but I'll be a good girl.

***

Cammie had met her group of friends in college

nearly ten years ago. They stayed in touch and met as often as varying schedules and geographical locations allowed. Today marked a sort of anniversary for the group, and as such, the day had been booked well in advance. Plans were made, and schedules were changed. Everyone was going to be there—all six of them. Cammie had excitedly squashed herself into her car with five other bodies. They were loud. They were happy, and they had already started to drink. Normally, Cammie would be first to crack open a bottle of wine, but her conscience hounded her.

Liam, Josie, and Cammie had discussed this part of their agreement. In fact, they had discussed a couple of things, but they had wanted to ensure that Cammie looked after herself, even if they couldn't always be there.

They hadn't signed a contract, but there had to be some structure laid out to keep Cammie in line when she wasn't with them. She had made a promise to try and adhere to their rules. It was for her own good, she knew.

However, Cammie felt justified in her choices, given that she was still a grown adult capable of making her own choices.

Cammie was enjoying her evening but became visibly uncomfortable when they reached the bar, and her eyes fell on her ex. It hadn't ended amicably. He had been her Daddy, but later she learned he was in it only for the sex and nothing else. She had lost her trust in people. More importantly, she had started to hate that she needed to be taken care of.

"Hey, little girl." His drawl sent a shiver up her spine. "Shouldn't you be in bed by now?" The double meaning was crystal clear, and it turned her stomach. Kain knew which buttons to push to irritate her.

Liz, who had heard the entire exchange, hooked her arm through Cammie's and pushed through the crowd ahead of them. The force of jostling people out of the way had caused another patron to stumble over his already unsteady footing and spilled his drink over Kain.

As was the norm where alcohol flowed deep and

emotions were left unchecked. A fistfight broke out.

The pair kept pushing through the crowd and disappeared among the writhing mass of hot bodies to where their friends were waiting with yet another tray of drinks. They seemed to have managed to recruit a waiter to serve them all night.

Cammie looked at the tray of shots in front of her. At the start of the evening, she had expressed her wish to avoid alcohol, claiming an early shift the next day. Now, however, as she came face to face with the pink, strawberry-flavored liqueur, her willpower faltered.

The echo of Josie's warning angered her this time. Why shouldn't she drink? It wasn't as if they were here. She was an adult. She kept reminding herself.

With a bratty sort of stubbornness, she shot the liquid down her throat and tapped the glass on the table. The girls cheered and did the same.

Steadily, more shots and cocktails appeared on their table as well as in Cammie's hand. She had abandoned her conscience six drinks ago and was as loud and exuberant as her friends. They periodically returned to the dancefloor and jumped, gyrated, and threw their arms around as they lost themselves in the music and booze. Cammie felt relaxed and carefree.

There were no responsibilities at that moment; all that mattered was that she maintained her buzz.

It was close to four in the morning when they stumbled out of the club. Liz had called a cab, and they were waiting in the crisp early morning air for it to arrive. The rest had gone home hours ago.

Cammie waved and shouted greetings as Liz' cab pulled away, Liz hanging out of the window to wave back. When the cab disappeared around the corner, Cammie headed for her car.

The cool air had cleared her head a little, but it wasn't enough.

The warmth of the car and the fact that she had started to calm down was making her head spin a little more. Her car swerved onto the sidewalk, nearly missing a trash can. Cammie slowed down but continued driving. Her mind focused on getting home and straight to bed.

It wasn't until the lights painted the world blue and the siren's whoop cut through the fog in her brain that Cammie realized she hadn't quite driven as straight as she initially thought. Or as slow.

Fuck.

Even though the fog in her head was clouding her judgment, she could imagine Liam and Josie's disappointed faces clearly. Cammie's stomach turned unhappily.

Over the sound system came the booming voice of God - or so Cammie thought it sounded - and asked her to put both her hands out of the window. She did as she was told. There was a click, and the seconds trickled by like molasses through the eye of a needle. Agonizingly slow. Her head was spinning, and a new kind of uneasiness settled in the pit of her stomach. One that had nothing to do with the fact that she had been pulled over.

"Ma'am, have you been drinking?" It was standard questions, but Cammie knew the officer hadn't needed to ask. The alcohol vapor was coming off of her in waves.

Cammie blinked at him, stupidly, "No?" Her lie was obvious, but she couldn't help it.

"Ma'am, please step out of the vehicle." Cammie wanted to argue, but her brain was struggling with the concept. She slowly opened the door from the outside. The latch clicked, and then her stomach lurched.

Oh no. No.

Cammie pushed the door open and-

The officer barely had enough time to step back as the contents of her stomach splashed on the ground.

***

Cammie woke to the sound of metal clanging on metal. Her eyes were gummed shut, and her mouth tasted like sewage. Her head pounded as she sat up carefully, too fragile to move too quickly. Nauseatingly bright light streamed through the high window, indicating that she had been there for most of the night.

The offending sound was coming from the slightly older-looking officer unlocking her cell, "Come on, time to sort this out."

The officer was polite and didn't touch her or talk too loud. He gave her a small smile, "We deal differently, miss. Just be sure this is what you want to be stuck with for the rest of your life."

Cammie stood close enough to read his name tag, or at least, after a few tries, she did manage to read it: Leo White successfully.

He indicated down the passage and stepped aside so that Cammie could get past him. Leo led her through the back of the station and set her down in front of a young officer that looked much too eager to be working this early in the morning, "Please wait right here, miss."

She sat in an uncomfortable chair, fidgeting. This early on a Monday morning, there wasn't much activity, but she still felt as though a million eyes were on her. At least she wasn't handcuffed. Perhaps it was the utter look of defeat on her face or the fact that her short stature set them at ease. Whatever the reason, Cammie was grateful. She wasn't sure that her self-esteem could take a blow like that.

That is until Josie walked into the room. There was a flicker of recognition before the anger and disappointment set in. Cammie knew what she must've looked like: smeared mascara, disheveled, and she probably still smelled like stale smoke and booze. Sleeping it off in the drunk tank didn't exactly come with shower privileges.

Josie approached the desk and addressed the officer busy feeding her information into the system, "Who's representing her?"

"We're still processing her details. W-we haven't called-"

Cammie was glad that the look she gave him was not aimed in her direction, although she was sure there would be time enough for that later. Josie looked over the docket that the now sweating officer had handed her. She went still. It was one thing to see Cammie in the police station, but to see those three letters inked onto the page caused anger to freeze her veins.

"No matter," Josie said, handing back the file. "I'll arrange for representation."

"Yes, ma'am." The officer, relieved that the irritation was short-lived, continued hammering the keys.

"Send her to my office once you are done. We'll read the charges when her lawyer gets here." When Josie looked at Cammie again, the anger had softened. It wasn't gone, but at least Cammie felt that she wasn't hated.

Josie had given Cammie some baby wipes to clean off her face, and some gum to help kill the gritty and gross feeling that lingered in her mouth.

When Liam had gotten the call from Josie, he could hardly believe it. First, he was furious. Then he started to think about what could have happened. He stepped through the door on that early Monday morning, and his eyes searched for her.

A silence hung between the three of them.

Cammie stared at her shoes, picking at her nails.

The polish, showing a nervous habit, chipped

and peeled in several places.

Liam tried to keep his voice low, and he did so by

sheer force of will. It wouldn't do to yell at her.

She had broken the rules. It wasn't even that.

She had put herself and others at risk. He was

torn between berating her as a lawyer and

comforting her as her Daddy. But she had broken

the rules, and she had to be punished. First, by

the law - there was no way out of it - and then by

Liam and Josie.

"I was stupid," Cammie said, still not

looking at either of them.

"No," Josie interjected. "You may have

done a stupid thing, but it doesn't mean you are

stupid."

Cammie had no reply.

Liam inhaled a deep breath and let it out slowly.

"Alright, so this is what's going to

happen," Liam said and proceeded to run

through the events as they would play out. "You will plead guilty, and then we will go to trial."

"What? Why?" Cammie looked up, surprised, and angry.

"You *are* guilty, Cammie," Liam stressed. "You could have hurt someone. You could have hurt yourself."

"Cammie, sweetheart. Something like this can't just be swept away. You need to understand that there will always be consequences for your actions." Josie's voice was kind but firm. Cammie looked at her as tears welled in her eyes and nodded.

"The plea hearing is in," Liam checked his watch, "three hours."

"I smell like a dirty ashtray and liquor; I can't show up like this. They've impounded my car." Cammie's voice was thick with emotion and anger.

"I slept in a jail cell and look like something the cat dragged in. How am I supposed to-" Cammie abruptly stopped taking when the frustration brought on tears. She hadn't really hoped that she would get away with it, but faced with the sudden realization that she was in serious trouble had caused anxiety to knot painfully in the pit of her stomach.

Liam contemplated for a brief moment whether that would be fitting punishment but then chastised himself. She needed to face the consequences, not be humiliated. He sighed, "We'll get you cleaned up."

Josie called for Leo, and in the few moments that followed, the room was silent.

"Yes, ma'am?" Leo said.

"Could you kindly stand in as Miss Chase's police escort for the afternoon until her plea hearing?"

"Yes, ma'am." Leo beckoned to Cammie, "Ready when you are, Miss."

Cammie was silently grateful for the friendly face as he led her out of the building.

Leo had made polite conversation as they headed down to her apartment in his police cruiser.

Cammie had taken a quick shower, dressed in a black dress she wore for a formal work function, and at Josie's request packed a few extra things into her bag.

Cammie tried to keep it together. Her world was slowly falling apart around her. Maybe Kain had been right. Cammie felt as alone right now as she had the day he had called her a needy, bratty, slut, and walked out of her life.

"Are you okay, Miss?" Leo asked, his eyes crinkling with concern.

Cammie nodded, steeled herself, and locked her apartment door behind her. It would be tomorrow's problem.

***

"Do you have family in the city?"

"No, sir- Your Honor," Cammie corrected herself and felt her cheeks burn.

After a moment of deliberation, the Judge shuffled the papers in front of him and called the council to the bench.

"Mr. Everhart, your client may have a job in the city, but since she has no relations or other ties here, I am inclined to keep her locked up until trial."

"Your Honor, I will personally see to it that she shows up to the hearing. She can post bail. She has no priors." Liam said quietly.

"With all due respect, counselor, your client is a danger to herself and others. She admitted guilt-"

"To making a mistake."

"Enough." The Judge held up his hand. "Mr. Everhart, can you with certainty say that the defendant will not fail to appear at her hearing?"

Liam considered this. Cammie needed a firm hand, that was certain, but she had not proven to be the type to run away simply. She may have hated to be in a situation that she herself created, but Cammie had accepted the consequences as they were.

"Yes, your Honor."

"Will you take responsibility?"

"Yes, your honor."

The Judge peered at him with eyes that seemed

to take in every inch of his soul, and with a wave
of his hand, dismissed them.

The Judge addressed the room, and Liam
noticed how Cammie's back straightened just a
little.

"Guilty. Bail is set at a thousand-two-
hundred dollars. Miss Chase, I am releasing you
into Mr. Everhart's care. Sentencing is scheduled
for ten days from today."

Chapter 5

The car ride home was painfully quiet. Cammie hadn't dared to say a word. It was one thing to disobey the rules set out by Liam and Josie, but it was quite another to break the law.

Cammie knew she had screwed up royally. In all honesty, she was waiting for Liam to drive her to her tiny apartment and leave her there, essentially nullifying their agreement.

She was still on probation with them. *Maybe not for long*, Cammie thought. Cammie wasn't keen on finding out where Liam and Josie stood with her, so she remained silent, listening to Liam breathe.

When they pulled up in front of Liam's house, Cammie looked at him in surprise, her mouth wanting to form words, but her brain refusing to supply them.

"Upstairs, now," Liam demanded, putting the car in park. "I'll be up in a minute. Josie is already waiting for us."

Cammie slid out of the car and let herself into

the house, trying to make as little noise as possible. The front door was unlocked, and the interior was dead quiet. The bright light of the living room guiding her like a beacon in the storm. The second Cammie saw Josie with her back to the door. Her throat went dry. Cammie stood awkwardly in the threshold between the living room and the kitchen, clutching her one arm close to her body. She heard the door close behind her, and Liam joined Josie in the kitchen.

Cammie could barely breathe as the stress gnawed at her, their eyes looking right through her.

"Cammie." It was all he had to say. Cammie knew there was going to be a discussion about the events of the past few days. The one thing that she hadn't shared with them was that she tended to lose control when alcohol was involved. It was a coping mechanism, a crappy one to be sure, but still. Liam and Josie were both standing in the kitchen, a chair had been pulled out for her, and they waited. Taking a deep breath, Cammie shuffled towards them and sat down. Her heart was in her throat, and her face was burning from shame.

"Cammie, what happened?" Cammie had expected Josie to be furious, shouting at her, but she wasn't. Her voice was calm, and Cammie thought, concerned.

Cammie had kept it together since the police station, but the second she opened her mouth to speak, the stress broke her. Cammie dropped her head in her hands and cried. Sobs wracked her whole body, shaking her, stealing the breath from her lungs, and causing her to sob harder. Liam and Josie shared a look of concern. It seemed to them that Cammie had been holding on to whatever it was that was eating away at her.

Josie wrapped her arms around Cammie, letting the girl's tears drip and soak into her blouse, "Everything will be okay, honey. I promise." Cammie sobbed harder, and for what seemed like an eternity, Cammie clutched at Josie and cried from the depths of her soul. When her sobs quieted, and her body stopped shaking, Cammie wiped at her eyes and face and looked up at Josie's waiting form.

They still expected some kind of explanation, and Cammie knew, the punishment was non-optional.

Cammie took a steadying breath, and tested her voice, cleared her throat and tried again, "Are you mad at me?"

A brief pause.

"We were, little one, but only because we were scared." Josie reached out and wiped a stray tear from her face, "Mommy and Daddy want to help you, but you need to tell us everything, Cammie."

"Okay, Mommy."

And so, she did. Cammie told them what had happened, including the part about her vomiting over a police officer's shoes. Liam and Josie were respectful, listening to her whole story before they asked their next questions.

"Who is Kain?" Liam asked, a slight edge to his voice. The longer he listened to Cammie explain her past relationship and how Kain had treated her, the angrier he got. He kept it in check, however, and the whole mess was eventually unloaded.

Cammie had laid bare absolutely everything about herself to these two people. She was vulnerable but relieved. Now, she thought, it's up to them if they still want her or not.

"I'm sorry, Mommy. Daddy." Cammie was close to tears again, "I made a bad choice, and it got me into so much trouble, and I was worried this whole time that you would be too angry ever to want to talk to me again."

"Little mouse, we're not going to abandon you for making a mistake," Liam said, "but you have to own up to them."

"Everything you do has a consequence, Cammie," Josie said, her face serious, but the kindness never leaving her voice.

Cammie nodded mutely, still wiping tears from her face.

"Cammie, you've been a bad girl," Josie said.

"Yes, Mommy."

"What did you do?"

"I broke the rules."

"Which rules did you break, Cammie?" Liam prompted.

Cammie swallowed, still feeling a little fragile, "I disobeyed Mommy."

"What else?"

"I drank alcohol, and I'm not allowed to," Cammie said. Once the words were out, the rest followed, "I drove a car while being drunk, and I put other people in danger. I lied, and I ignored messages from Mommy and Daddy." Cammie breathed shakily, but let everything flow out. It was cathartic in a way, to come clean. Confessing her sins and secrets had released a part of her, she hadn't realized she was holding on to.

"That's right," Josie said.

"What happens when you break the rules, little mouse?"

Cammie looked at the two of them where they stood in the kitchen and felt a warmth spread through her. She knew she messed up, but they weren't angry at her. She had disappointed them, but they did not shout or raise their voices. They allowed her to tell her story, her version of events, not the black and white paragraphs of the docket, and they were still kind towards her.

"I get punished."

"Do you understand why we have to punish you?" Josie asked. Cammie nodded. Their caring manner made her feel less like a failure and more like someone who simply needed proper guidance. Her vulnerability was exposed, and Cammie waited. Liam and Josie were exactly the kind of people she needed in her life. They could provide her the stability she so desperately needed. Cammie knew she needed a firm hand. Liam and Josie knew that too.

"Use your big girl words, Cammie." Liam prompted, his voice still low.

"Yes, Mommy." Cammie finally answered Josie's question.

"Good girl. Now, follow Daddy, please." Liam held out his hand to Cammie, and she took it, grateful for the contact. She followed him to a room up another flight of stairs. It was pleasantly decorated but had chains attached to the bed, along with a wall-mounted display of whips, paddles, and other paraphernalia. Cammie swallowed.

Liam led her to the bed and told her to bend over. She was still dressed in the modest dress she wore for the hearing.

She did as Liam asked, and he lifted the hem of her dress over her bottom, exposing the pink undies she had bought on the day they had run into each other.

He had made a show of choosing a large, wooden paddle. It was thick and had etchings carved into the handle. Liam placed the cool wood against Cammie's ass and held it there for a time.

Cammie quivered in anticipation.

Liam did not ask her to count this time.

Whack.

Whack. Whack. Whack.

After a few harder blows, Liam would pause to run the paddle against her bottom. He didn't say a word as he punished her. Cammie had started to squirm and squeak softly as the blows landed.

"Daddy?" Cammie asked when a particularly hard hit caused her eyes to water, "Daddy, can we stop, please?"

Again, Liam did not speak, but he did set the paddle down to stroke Cammie's ass. He slid her panties down, and the coolness of the air against her skin brought a moment of relief. Cammie let out a shaky breath.

"Stand up, little one," Liam commanded, and Cammie obeyed, her eyes wide. Liam smiled reassuringly, "You'll be okay, little mouse."

"Remember, we'll stop when you tell us to," Josie said.

Cammie nodded. Her eyes were still wide, but she trusted them. Cammie had been asked to undress. She did so while both Liam and Josie watched.

"Come here, little girl." Josie held out a set of thick, leather cuffs, with a very short chain between them. "Turn around."

Cammie did and held perfectly still, and Josie cuffed her arms together behind her back, "Good girl."

Liam had exchanged the paddle for a thin spanking whip with a flared tip. Josie had gently made Cammie bend over the bed again, her ass in the air, legs apart.

When the first blow landed, Cammie let out a squeak of surprise. It hadn't hurt nearly as much as she had anticipated, but the thin leather felt very different from the wooden paddle she was used to.

Liam made her count. One, loud, hard, *whack* for every day of her sentence. By the time the thirtieth spank came around, Cammie was panting. Both from the pain and the pleasure of it.

"Do you understand why you're being punished, baby girl?" Liam asked as he loosened his tie.

"Yes, Daddy. I'm sorry, Daddy."

Josie took the opportunity to work a small, silicone butt plug into her ass hole. Cammie squirmed and voiced her distress at having something penetrating her there.

"You know the words to make us stop, little girl. Any time it gets too much." Liam whispered in her ear as he stood in front of Cammie, his cock hard and standing at attention.

"Open your mouth, Cammie." Liam wrapped his fingers through her hair and held her steady as she sucked on his dick. Cammie jerked in surprise as a thick cock spread her pussy lips so far apart that she felt as though she was going to break in two. She pulled away from Liam and strained to see behind her. Josie had a thick dildo strapped onto her and was slowly working its thick head into her already soaked pussy.

Cammie came multiple times as both Liam and Josie stretched her to her limits. Still, she did not protest. Even though some of it hurt, Cammie felt safe enough to know that they would not seriously hurt her.

***

Liam undid the straps on the cuffs around

Cammie's wrists, gently massaging blood flow back into her arms and fingers, "How do you feel, Cammie?"

"I-" Cammie paused, mentally running a hand over her body and assessing her emotions. "I'm sore, Daddy."

"What can I do to make my little girl feel better?" Liam asked, still running his fingers over her wrists and arms.

"I want a hug," Cammie said, "and a bubble bath."

"How about a warm bottle and cuddles while we watch some TV after?" Liam suggested as he effortlessly lifted Cammie onto his lap. Cammie sank into his body, absorbing the warmth and closeness of her Daddy's touch. Liam rocked her gently, listening to her breathing. When she was ready, Cammie pulled away slightly and asked him to carry her to her bathroom, where Josie had already prepared a hot bubble bath for her.

"Would you like Mommy to bathe you, or me?" Liam asked as he set the girl down on the toilet seat.

"Mommy," Cammie said as she reached up for Josie.

"What do we say?" Liam prompted.

"Please, will you stay with me, Mommy?"

"Of course, my sweetheart," Josie said. Liam closed the door behind them, listening to the girls' chatter and splash as they cleaned up. By the time they had finished, Liam had already made a giant pile of blankets and pillows on the living room floor. Josie and Cammie made themselves comfortable, snuggling close together. Liam was surprised by how different Cammie was compared to the other Littles they had cared for. She seemed to require more physical touch while some others preferred a quick cuddle and alone time.

"Here you go, little mouse," Liam said and handed her a baby bottle filled with strawberry flavored milk.

"Thank you, Daddy." Cammie said and snuggled into Josie's heavy chest, "Can we please watch My Little Pony?"

"Whatever you want, little mouse."

And that's how they spent the remainder of the night. Cammie snuggled between Liam and Josie, as she animatedly described each of the characters and their backstories in great detail. The show was still running when Cammie had fallen asleep with her head on Liam's chest. Not wanting to disturb her, Liam and Josie had simply stayed with her, talking quietly as the colorful ponies went on their friendship adventures.

Chapter 6

The following morning Liam had taken Cammie to work. Her car had been impounded, and since he was responsible for the girl until her hearing, it only made sense that he drive her. Cammie's mood had only marginally improved. She shifted uncomfortably in the passenger seat. Her bottom was still tender after the punishment last night.

"Thank you, Daddy, for driving me to work again."

"It's no trouble, sweetheart."

***

Josie had been going over Cammie's paperwork, ensuring that the docket was as complete as possible. All new information had been fed into the system and added to her file. Josie looked up from her papers just as Liam rapped a knuckle on the doorframe of her office, "Got a minute?"

"Anything for you, Liam." Her smile was

genuine, and he shut the door behind him, "Is there something specific I can help with, or is this a social call?" The playful twinkle in Josie's eyes told him she didn't make a distinction between the two.

The woman was insatiable. With a returning grin, he said, "Definitely not the time or place, Josie." They shared a laugh as he kissed her cheek, half-falling, half-sitting in the old gray couch across from the desk.

"It's about Cammie," he said. "I think the girl needs-" he paused to find just the right word, "more permanent supervision."

Josie didn't look at all surprised at his suggestion, "Permanently? As in, permanently with us?"

"Yes."

"What if she isn't interested, Liam?"

"Look at how well she responded to us last night, Josie. She needs structure and permanence."

"I agree that she needs the structure," Josie said and leaned forward in her chair, swiveling closer to him, "but we need to be sure that it is what she would want. We can't force her, no matter the dynamic between us. She's still a fully grown adult."

Liam took in her words. Josie was right, of course, but that didn't mean he wasn't going to try. He told Josie exactly that, and they began discussing the details.

"There's one more thing we need to consider here, Liam," Josie said seriously, "We need to consider the possibility that Cammie won't agree to any of this."

"I am aware of that, Josie."

"I want to take care of her, too, Liam." There was a long moment of silence as Liam mulled over her words, and his mind worked through multiple scenarios.

"How about a trial run, then?" Josie finally said.

Liam sat forward, suddenly a little more lively, "It would be perfect. You're a genius, Josie."

"It's why you married me," Josie said with a wink.

***

At the end of Cammie's shift, she found Liam already in the parking lot waiting for her. She waved excitedly and hopped in the passenger side, "Hi, Daddy!"

"Hi, little mouse. How was your day?" Cammie took off, talking about the job, the people, and the customers. When Cammie noticed that her voice was getting to be a little louder than she had intended, she stopped short and lowered her voice, "Sorry, Daddy."

"Do you hate your job?" Liam asked, not wanting her to stop talking yet.

"I don't really hate it, but it just drains me sometimes, you know?" Cammie stared ahead and watched the light change from red to green. As Liam pulled away, she added, "I sometimes do like it, but it's not what I had wanted to do for this long. It was just supposed to be a stepping stone."

"Have you thought about quitting?"

"I can't really afford to even if I wanted to," Cammie said honestly. She had debts and rent. Not to mention, the bail money she had paid had left a giant hole in her bank account, which was yet another thing she would need to worry about.

"What would you like to do?" Liam asked probing. Cammie thought for a moment, and a smile broke over her face. *She really is a lovely girl*, Liam thought as he stole glances. Cammie spent the greater part of the ride home talking about her dreams.

Liam made the appropriate noises for her to continue the conversation, but otherwise, simply let her talk. The passion he saw burning in her eyes made him absolutely certain that Cammie would be great with the two of them.

"Josie and I want to discuss something with you," Liam said as they pulled up to the house, and Cammie's story came to a close.

"What is it?"

"Let's go inside. We can discuss it there." Cammie threw her arms around Josie as she stepped into the living room, inhaling her warm scent. She felt safe here.

"We know you have a lot going on at the moment, Cammie. Especially after the latest developments."

Cammie cringed at the memory, and her stomach turned. *I am never drinking again.* "It's been a little hectic," she agreed.

"What is it?" Cammie asked, seeing him hesitate.

"Please, understand that you shouldn't feel obligated in any way," Josie said.

"We want you to move in with us. Permanently." Liam offered.

***

Cammie had accepted their offer without much thought. She hated living alone but could never quite bring herself to get a roommate.

In a short amount of time, they had gone from strangers to friends to family. Cammie could hardly believe her luck. Here she was, a college dropout, finding her place with two of the most amazing humans she knew.

They had already shared so much of themselves with each other, both physically and mentally. Cammie didn't have to think about it, because she knew it was what she had been looking for.

It took just one day for Cammie to have her apartment cleared out and her things brought over. The three of them sat at the kitchen counter with a stack of paperwork in front of them. It took a while as they worked through each part of the document Liam had drawn up. Whatever wasn't understood was explained and rephrased to make the meaning clear. The document covered everything from her chosen safe words, fantasies, and triggers down to public displays and outright bondage.

They had set out the ground rules and the punishments attached should they be broken. Cammie agreed with most and asked for changes to be made to some things that she hadn't quite yet felt comfortable with.

This led to the creation of a detailed list of her personal limits. Some, like participating in anal sex was a soft limit for her, while others such as blood play were completely off the table.

Cammie agreed to wear whatever they chose for her outside of her work uniform. For the duration of her community service, she would be forced to wear a butt plug and diaper at all times unless permission was given for removal.

In turn, they each signed the contract once they were satisfied with its contents.

Cammie felt giddy. It was the start of something great.

Chapter 7

Liam, Josie, and Cammie stood in the doorway of the spare bedroom, looking at the empty space. The three of them had cleared out the furniture and decorations in preparation for Cammie moving in with them.

"Can we paint one wall egg-shell blue?" Cammie asked as she saw Josie hold up what looked like paint samples against the stark white walls.

"Maybe, but let's see what other colors we have, too," Josie said and beckoned Cammie over. Together they looked through the stack of color tabs.

"What about this one?" Josie prompted. It was a light green. The label said it was a lime milkshake color, but Cammie giggled and shook her head.

"Noooo," Cammie said adamantly.

"Why not?" Josie said, surprised by

Cammie's reaction.

"It looks like a nose boogie," Cammie whispered conspiratorially, still giggling.

"Cammie!" Josie scolded but laughed. She had to agree. The color was definitely not as nice as it had seemed a few minutes ago. Josie discarded the color tab and lined up the remaining five.

And so they worked their way through their final choices and settled on two. A sunshine yellow (which Cammie was so excited about that she nearly ran Liam over when they went to show him) and a dark, muted purple. They also decided to use a light gray as an accent color. Cammie had spent the week practicing how to draw a mouse and went to show Josie when she finally managed to make it look the way she had wanted it to.

"Mommy?" Cammie asked as Josie looked over the drawing Cammie had given her.

"Yes, my sweet?"

"Can-can I paint that on my wall?"

Cammie had expected Josie to deny her request

outright, but by the smile on her face, Cammie felt hope rise and bubble in her chest.

"Do you want me to help, or can you do it by yourself?"

"I'm- I'm allowed to paint by myself?" Cammie asked incredulously.

"Yes, you adorable little mouse," Josie said and hugged her tightly. "It's your room, and we can decorate it however you want."

***

Cammie stood enthralled in front of the wall of plushies. Her eyes darted from one plushie to the other. The colors were overwhelming, and she found herself touching each one, feeling the fur under her fingertips.

"Mommy?" Cammie said softly, tugging on the hem of her blouse.

"Yes, sweetheart?" Josie had been watching her as the girl took in every detail. She could see the twinkle of sheer joy in her eyes as they darted from one fuzzball to the next.

"I don't know which one to choose." Her voice was small and sounded as though it was about to break.

"It's okay, Cammie," Josie reassured her and squeezed her shoulders. "Take your time."

"Okay, Mommy." Cammie's tension drifted away, and she started picking up plushies and holding them to her. After some time passed, she would either place them in a pile at her feet or return them to the shelf. Josie watched, her heart filling with joy.

"Are you having fun, little one?" Josie asked.

Cammie was distracted as she stared intently at the plushie in her hands. It was a gray mouse as big as her torso and nearly as wide. It was fat and round, with small pink hands and feet.

When the girl had made up her mind, she spun to face Josie, her eyes full of tears, "I want this one!" Cammie was shaking. The stuffie was large, soft, and cute. Her heart was breaking at the thought of Josie saying no, and she could barely keep her tears in check.

"Are you sure, little girl?"

Cammie nodded vigorously, causing some of her butterfly clips to come undone. Josie wrapped her arm around the girl and pulled her close, kissing the top of her head, "Go show Daddy, little one."

Cammie was off like a rocket. She found him only two aisles over where he was measuring the size of a very large bed with rails made of thick wood. It stood high off of the ground and looked to be hand-carved. A small ladder attached to each side allowed the user to climb into the bed comfortably.

"Daddy, look!" Cammie held the fat stuffie in front of his face, "It's a mouse! Isn't he cute?" Liam gasped and dramatically held his heart, "Goodness! A mouse for my little mouse." Cammie giggled and held the stuffie close to her chest as if she was afraid that someone would make her return it to its place on the shelf.

"Why don't you go give it to the cashier by the front counter?" Liam suggested. Cammie hesitated, but Liam smiled, the softness of the action crinkling the corners of his eyes, "We have to pay for it, darling. The cashier can ring it up in the meantime. You don't have to leave it there." The kindly cashier nodded in her direction, and Cammie did as Liam had said. Cammie felt her heart thump wildly in her chest as the cashier handed the fat mouse back to her after just a few seconds.

"So, I can keep this?" Cammie asked the man.

"Of course, little one," Josie said as she dropped off a handful of colorful sheets. "These as well, thank you, Ed."

"No problem, Ms. Josie."
Cammie shouted in elation and whizzed away, running through the aisles to look at the rest of the things the store had to offer.

***

"There you are!" Josie called. Cammie was quietly sitting in one of the small plastic chairs in the corner as Liam and Josie had gone about

their shopping spree. Cammie had lost interest
after the first hour.

"I got tired, Mommy," Cammie said, still
clutching her new stuffie.

"It's okay, little girl. Let's go home."

***

When Cammie returned from work the next day,
Liam had already installed the crib, and the
room was lit by soft lighting coming from a lamp
on a matching end table.

"Woooow." Cammie breathed. The room
looked exactly like she had imagined. She saw
that Josie had carefully placed Meekie on her
pillow as if it were waiting for Cammie to return
home.

"What do you think, Cammie?" Liam
asked as he stood in the doorway, watching her
admire the room.

"I love it, Daddy." Cammie threw her arms
around him, pressing herself against his already
hardening cock.

"Daddy?" Cammie asked, her eyes dark with heat

"Yes, little one?"

"I want you to touch me, Daddy," Cammie said, taking his hand and pressing it firmly between her legs. She rubbed herself against his fingers, "When will Mommy be home? I want her to be here too."

As if on cue, they heard keys jangle in the lock.

"Mommy!"

Cammie ambushed Josie before she had made it halfway across the living room, "I want us to play together, Mommy."

Josie met Liam's gaze, saw the bulge in his pants, and grinned, "Ambushed you first?"

Liam laughed and nodded.

"Well, then, little girl. Why don't you come help Mommy change into something more comfortable?" Josie said, pulling her along by the hand.

"You should come too, Daddy," she added and winked at Liam.

Chapter 8

Cammie had chosen the same dress she had worn for her plea hearing. It was also quite possibly the only modest dress she owned, which made getting ready that morning pretty straightforward. Despite being ready to leave an hour before they were scheduled to show, Cammie had nervously straightened her dress and messed with her hair.

In the car, she couldn't sit still, fidgeting as Liam drove them to see the courthouse.

It wouldn't be a big trial that involved a jury, at least, and for that, Cammie was grateful. So far, she had managed to keep her private life private, especially from her employers. It would be horrifying if she lost her job because of something she could have prevented.

It was the same Judge they had seen for the plea hearing. He looked as surly as ever, and Cammie took a steadying breath.

The charges against Cammie were laid out, and in turn, the sentencing was discussed. Liam had discussed with her the potential outcomes of the hearing today. From best case scenario to worst. Cammie had become pale when he explained to her that the chance existed that she could be sentenced to time behind bars.

Without getting her hopes up, Liam had also discussed with her the reasonable expectations given that it was a first-time offense. Cammie had only nodded, unable to speak.

Now, however, while they were arguing back and forth, Cammie had a host of questions bubbling up inside of her, making her heart pound loudly in her ears. Cammie knew there was no point in asking them now. What would happen would happen.

"Your Honor," Liam interjected, "The officers had no valid reason to pull her over. They didn't follow the procedure. My client's sobriety wasn't tested before they took her into custody."

"She was driving erratically, Your Honor." Liam's opponent all but shouted and stomped his foot like a petulant child. Cammie could see the vein in his neck throbbing. The opposition was going out of his way to get an extended sentence for her, and perhaps even jail time. Liam was flouting his every argument and laying out his own.

The Judge, to his credit, was listening intently. Cammie, on the other hand, couldn't help her mind wandering. She knew she ought to be paying attention, but the nervous energy kept her from hearing much over the buzz in her ears. The room had gone quiet, which snapped Cammie back to reality. The Judge was looking at her as if he was waiting for a response to a question. The look on Liam's face sent a chill down his spine. She wasn't helping his case by not paying attention.

"Miss Chase?" The Judge looked annoyed, and Cammie swallowed.

"I'm sorry, Your Honor, I didn't quite catch the question," Cammie said, avoiding Liam's gaze, feeling her face burn.

"Are you willing to accept full responsibility for your actions, Miss Chase?" The

Judge repeated.

Cammie did look at Liam then and saw him give her the slightest of nods. "Yes, Your Honor."

"Mr. Everhart has set up quite the compelling defense. However," he shuffled through his notes. He stared down at something through his tiny spectacles balancing on the tip of his nose, "the fact remains that you *were* operating a motor vehicle while under the influence of alcohol. The blood tests confirm that allegation despite improper procedures." Cammie waited quietly for the Judge to continue.

"It is not a matter we take lightly, Miss Chase, and neither should you. While no major damage was done, you put others at risk through your selfish actions."

"Yes, Your Honor." Dread settled in her stomach. Perhaps she was going to go to jail after all.

"After reviewing your case, I am sentencing you to thirty days community service. I am also ordering you to attend Alcoholics Anonymous meetings during the same time period."

That was it: no gavel, no ceremony, and no more arguments. The Judge shoved the papers into a binder, set it aside, and motioned for the bailiff to bring forward the next case.

Liam guided Cammie out of the courtroom, his face unreadable. He cordially shook the hand of his opponent, and they went their separate ways. Cammie and Liam returned to his car. Again, the ride home was made in silence.

***

Cammie had taken the day off work to attend the sentencing hearing. Liam had dropped her off at home and with a reassuring hug, returned to work.

She wandered aimlessly through the house, frustrated. As part of the deal, Josie had removed any and all alcohol from the house. She needed to take the edge off. Cammie had scoured every inch of the house before falling into the couch with a loud sigh.

Cammie was ashamed. At last, the realization hit her. *I need to make some permanent changes in my life,* Cammie thought. Time passed slowly, but Cammie remained on the couch, eventually drifting off to sleep.

When she woke, Cammie felt better and prepared for Liam and Josie's return by taking a bath. A bubble bath never failed to lighten her mood.

***

Liam and Josie had called a family meeting, and as before, the three of them sat at the kitchen counter.

"Liam told me how the hearing went," Josie said. "Which means, now we need to work out a new schedule for you, so you have enough time to do your chores."

"Yes, Mommy."

"Cammie, do you know how lucky you were in that courtroom today?" Liam asked, his gaze intense, and his lips drawn together tightly.

Cammie shook her head. Cammie was aware that she could have gone to jail for a few months but hadn't truly grasped how easily the Judge could have swung that way.

"Adams is spectacular at his job, and if he were facing off against anyone else, you could very well have ended up in the worst-case scenario, little one. You came off fairly light, given who we were up against today." Cammie's eyes grew wide, "I didn't know, Daddy."

"Which is why, Josie and I think that in order for you to truly understand how serious we are about you following the rules, we will be giving you our own version of punishment." Cammie grimaced and hugged her stuffie tighter. The fat little mouse had become a source of comfort to her that eased the ache of anxiety she felt when dealing with real-world problems.

"What are you going to do?" she asked.

"Starting right now, you will wear diapers and a butt plug every day."

"A what?" Cammie's voice was shrill. The

protest was more from disbelief than not understanding.

"Excuse me?"

Cammie mumbled an apology.

"You need to prove to us that you can be a good girl," Josie said.

"I *am* a good girl, Mommy."

Liam held up his hand and continued, "If you break more rules, the butt plug will stay in. If you obey the rules and prove that you are a good girl, we can take it out at night."

"And if we feel you aren't taking this seriously enough, the size of the butt plug will increase," Josie added.

"Do you understand, little mouse?"

Cammie nodded, then, "I understand, Daddy."

Chapter 9

The three of them had the following day off together. It was so rare that they hadn't quite realized it until Josie shot out of bed to attempt to wake Cammie for work. The clock read 8:39 AM. Cammie was sure to be late, even if she skipped breakfast.

"Cammie, honey, it's time to get up." Josie coaxed.

A tired and annoyed grumble made Josie climb into the bed with her. She crawled under the covers and gave Cammie a giant hug, stroking her hair.

"Come, little one. You'll be late."

Bleary-eyed, Cammie turned her head to look at Josie, "I don't have to get up today, Mommy."

"What about work? You'll get in trouble." Josie said firmly.

Cammie giggled softly, turned around completely, and snuggled up to Josie. It was warm and comfortable, and Josie smelled nice.

"I don't have work today." Cammie

yawned and fell right back asleep.

Josie lay there for a moment, silently laughing at herself. With a sigh of relief, Josie made to get up, but Cammie had wrapped her arms around her tightly, making small noises of protest with each attempt to dislodge them.

Josie surrendered and fell asleep. She only woke much later to the smell of cooking bacon. Her stomach grumbled, and she heard a muffled giggle. Josie opened her eyes to find Cammie staring at her, her hand in front of her mouth to silence her giggles.

"I'm sorry, Mommy. I didn't mean to wake you, but your tummy made me giggle so much."

"Is it growling again?" Josie asked in mock annoyance, rolling her eyes for added effect.

Cammie giggled again just as another loud gurgle spoke up from beneath the sheets.

"I can hear you two giggling in there," Liam called. "Better come get some breakfast before I eat it all, even the pancakes."

Cammie let out a loud shout and flailed, almost falling from the bed.

"Careful, little one. You could get hurt." Josie steadied her and helped her get down. Cammie giggled hysterically as she ran ahead, "I want pancakes, Daddy!"

***

Cammie had stubbornly attempted to help them clean up, despite Liam stopping her. Cammie had grabbed her plate and ran to the sink. She lost her footing and dropped the plate. It shattered with a loud crash.
Cammie stood among the mess, her heart hammering in her chest. She burst into tears, sinking to her knees, "I'm sorry, I'm sorry, please don't be mad."

"Cammie, I told you not to." Liam's voice was deep and heavy. Cammie's heart shrank, and she cried harder.
They got the mess cleaned up, and when Cammie had calmed down, Josie had punished her for

disobeying Liam. As usual, the punishment turned into play and eventual sexual release for all three.

"Come, sweet little girl," Josie whispered as she held her hand out for Cammie. Josie had already loosened her bonds and was helping her stand. Cammie's footing was unsteady, and her eyes held a glazed, faraway look that pleased her. Josie helped Cammie to her adjoining bathroom and sat her down on the toilet seat. They murmured about her punishment and the play that followed.

Cammie looked at her knees and listened to the running water. When the temperature was just right, Josie kissed the top of Cammie's head, "Let's get you cleaned up."

Cammie hopped into the bath, sinking into the bubbles. Her bottom still stung a little, but the water was soothing. Cammie was spent. Emotionally and physically.

"Mommy?"

"Yes, Cammie?"

"You can get in with me," Cammie offered.

She could still see Josie's juices leaking from her swollen pussy. "The water is nice and warm."

"Do you think we'll both fit?" Josie asked, laughing slightly.

"Yes, Mommy!" Cammie splashed some water as she pulled her legs to her chest. Cammie wiggled excitedly as Josie stepped into the bath. There really was enough space for the two of them to sit comfortably.

After some time had passed, Cammie grabbed the large bottle of bath gel and held it out to Josie, "Please help me wash, Mommy."

"Alright. Turn around, baby."

Cammie shifted and tried to turn around too quickly, more water splashed out, causing the bathroom mat to get soaked, "Oops." Cammie giggled and finally managed to have her back facing Josie, with only a small amount of water making it onto the floor this time.

Josie glooped a sizable amount of body wash onto Cammie's duck-shaped bath sponge. Josie washed the girl's back and shoulders. When she was done, she made Cammie stand in the bath.

"Hold onto the hand railing, okay?" Josie
reminded her.

"Yes, Mommy." Cammie dutifully held
onto the safety rail and stood firmly, careful not
to shift her weight suddenly and lose her footing.
Standing in the tub was dangerous, and with the
added slipperiness of the bubble bath only added
to the danger.

Josie washed from the small of her back, running
the sponge over Cammie's ass. She saw the
redness was fading but was still gentle as she ran
the sponge over the area again. Then Josie ran
her hand between the girl's legs. Cammie
shivered, and Josie noted the way her thighs
quickly pressed together before she allowed her
to continue.

Cammie was still sensitive to touch after Liam's
punishment. Her body remembered the
sensation, and she felt new moisture between her
legs. Whether Josie noticed or not, she never let
on. She simply continued scrubbing.

Josie scrubbed Cammie's thighs and legs, then
rinsed her off with the sponge and water.

Cammie carefully turned around, still holding onto the safety rail. Josie refreshed the bath gel on the sponge and stood.

Josie lathered soap over Cammie's shoulders and arms, washing between each fold of her fingers and under her arms. She gently scrubbed around, under, and over Cammie's firm breasts. They were just enough for a handful. Cammie's nipples hardened under Josie's touch, but she kept scrubbing.

Josie sat back down in the bathtub. With one hand, she held onto Cammie's hip, and with the other, she lightly ran the sponge over her nether lips. The girl was clean-shaven, just the way Josie liked. It was a perk that Cammie had preferred it that way too.

Cammie's body was getting used to the sensation of the sponge and Josie's touch. It no longer quivered in anticipation, and Cammie sighed a silent sigh of relief. She wasn't sure if she would have been able to take any more torture.

Cammie sat down and lifted her one foot then the other. Josie scrubbed both, tickling her toes in the process. Cammie laughed and squirmed. More water splashed out. Liam knocked on the door and peeked inside, a hand over his eyes.

"How are my two favorite girls?" He asked.

"Mommy is tickling my feet!" Cammie laughed and squirmed some more.

"We're super, Liam," Josie said, smiling at how silly he looked with his hands over his eyes.

"I was thinking," Liam said, grinning, "we should have waffles and ice cream for dinner." Cammie was exuberant, "Yes, please, yes please, yes please!"
Josie laughed, "Apparently, that's a yes."

"Excellent. You two have fun, I'll get started on those waffles." With that, Liam closed the door, and they were left alone again.

***

Liam and Josie laughed as Cammie licked her plate clean, strawberry syrup, and melted ice cream smeared on her nose and one of her cheeks.

"Silly goose," Josie said and wiped Cammie's face with a cloth.

Liam cleared up the kitchen while Josie and Cammie, her belly stuffed full of waffles and ice cream, waddled to her nursery.

Cammie, with some effort and a boost from a chuckling Josie, hoisted herself up onto her bed. It also functioned as a crib, but Cammie only needed it when she slept restlessly.

"Can I have some cuddles?" Cammie asked as she hugged her stuffed mouse, Meekie, to her chest. Her eyes were growing a little heavy, but she didn't want to fall asleep yet. She needed the comfort Josie gave her and was afraid that Josie would get up as soon as she fell asleep.

"Sure thing, sweetheart." Josie hopped onto the bed with Cammie and took up position behind her, pulling her in tight. Josie squished her while Cammie laughed and squirmed.

"Alright, little one. Time to settle down now." Josie pulled a blanket over her and tucked her in, making sure that Meekie's head was outside of the blanket.

"Don't let Meekie suffocate, okay?"

"I won't." Cammie gave a great yawn and settled in as Josie wrapped her arms around her bundled form. She stroked her hair and hummed quietly.

"Mommy?"

"Yes, little one?"

"Thank you for being my Mommy," Cammie said and snuggled closer.
Josie felt a lump in her throat and squeezed the girl tighter, "Thank you for letting me, Cammie." It wasn't long before their evening's activities caught up with them, and they fell asleep. Liam came to check on them. He stood in the doorway for a long while, just watching them sleep.

"Good night, little mouse," he whispered as he tucked a strand of hair behind her ear. Both his girls were fast asleep as he pulled the door behind him. He left it open a crack.

Chapter 10

On her first day of community service, Cammie had stopped by the Community Center to get her job assigned for that day. Each day was the same. Go to the center, get her assignment for the day, and carry on with her job.

When her service had started, Liam had insisted that she keep wearing the diaper and butt plug, reminding her of the conditions attached. Cammie had occasionally taken it out when her shift had started, and then replaced it once her shift had ended before Liam came to collect her from work. So far, she had been careful and hadn't been caught. Cammie felt her heart race each time she took the butt plug out and stuffed it into her bag before starting her community service, or her shift at work. She knew Liam and Josie would be upset if they ever found out, but it was too big for her to get used to.

She had been helping out in the soup kitchen all of last week, and she had had the time to replace it before Liam would arrive to collect her.

Today, however, Liam had arrived early.

When he saw her, Liam noticed a slight change in her behavior. Cammie looked decidedly uneasy, and, a little guilty.

At first, Liam thought it was simply because he had arrived earlier than normal. Cammie had politely requested that he remain in his car at the end of her community service shift. Cammie hadn't wanted to be seen as a 'little rich girl.'

Liam was grateful that Cammie was attempting to socialize with the other people around her. It would be good to learn from their experiences. None of the other people in her group had done anything too serious, all misdemeanors, and all minors.

If Cammie was seen being picked up and dropped off in a large, pricey SUV, the other people in her group could turn hostile. Liam was familiar with the dynamic. He could see her point and had agreed.

Liam actually had a different motive for arriving earlier. He wanted to check in on her progress with her supervisor. As part of her agreement with the court, as well as with him, was that she would take this situation seriously.

Second chances didn't happen frequently.

The other court-mandated punishment was that Cammie had to attend Alcoholics Anonymous. Her emotional wellbeing was a top priority, and being sure that she was giving it her all would set his mind at ease.

There was no doubt that Cammie was taking it seriously. However, the girl had a tendency to revert to old habits. It was easier to just fall back on doing the bare minimum in order to get by. The new ground rules, as set out by their contract, enforced her full cooperation in legal matters. While Cammie was finishing up her shift, Liam and her supervisor chatted freely. Cammie tried to keep her face neutral when Liam greeted her, "How's my girl?"

"I'm fine."

Liam arched a brow at her, "Excuse me?"

"I'm sorry, Daddy. I'm okay. I'm just a little tired."

"Alright." Liam wrapped an arm around

her and gave her a side hug, "How about we stop for some ice cream on the way home, little mouse?"

The cloud behind her eyes broke, and she smiled, "Could we, please?"

Liam laughed as he opened the passenger door for her and helped her in, "Of course, little mouse."

The zipper on Cammie's bag hadn't been closed all the way, and as Cammie tossed it into the back seat, it fell on its side, allowing some of the contents to spill out. Cammie had been careless.

Cammie bounced excitedly in her seat, the dread of having her secret discovered forgotten, "Can I get more than one flavor, Daddy?"

Liam reached back to set it right side up to keep more things from flying out and saw it. Carefully wrapped in toilet paper was the large purple heart butt plug. Josie had chosen that one specifically for her.

As they reached the fast-food joint, Liam stopped the car in the parking lot, "Cammie, look at me."

"Yes, Daddy?" Cammie asked, still excited

about the prospect of ice cream, looking at him expectantly.

"Were you a good girl today?"

A heartbeat.

"Yes, Daddy." Cammie's eyes were still wide with excitement, unaware that Liam had found the butt plug.

"Is there something you'd like to tell me, Cammie?"

"No, Daddy."

"Are you sure?"

"Yes, Daddy." Her voice was softer now, and she had some trouble maintaining eye contact. Her face burned with embarrassment. Liam reached behind him and pulled the ball of toilet paper from the bag and held it out to her.

"Do you know what this is, little mouse?"

"No, Daddy."

Liam's eyes darkened, "Cammie, we have talked about lying. You know how I feel about it."

"Yes, Daddy."

Liam let the silence settle, wanting to see how far Cammie would go with her little game of pretend. Cammie refused to meet his gaze, squirming uncomfortably in her seat. Liam unfolded the little package. Slowly. Making sure Cammie saw every single move as he revealed the sparkly purple butt plug.

Cammie looked up at him from beneath her lashes. There was no way out of this now. Her face burned hotter, and her stomach churned.

"Is this yours, little mouse?"

"Yes, Daddy."

"Why aren't you wearing it?"

"It was uncomfortable, Daddy."

"Are you allowed to take it out?"

"No, Daddy."

Again Liam let the silence press in on them in the car. He could hear her strangled breathing and noted the tremble of her fingers as she laced and unlaced them in her lap. Liam placed the butt plug in her lap, and he started the car.

"Wait, Daddy!" Cammie said, looking back at the fast-food joint, longing in her eyes, "We didn't get ice cream."

"Ice cream is for good girls only, little

mouse," Liam noted the disappointment on her face and expected more of a fuss, but Cammie held her protests.

When they got home, Liam ordered Cammie to grab her things and wait for him in her room. Cammie had opened her mouth as if to argue, then nodded and quietly disappeared into the house.

"Cammie, you know I don't want to punish you."

"I know Daddy."

"But you've been a bad girl."

"Yes, Daddy."

"Please choose your punishment," Liam said, indicating the bedside table where they kept a variety of punishment tools.

"Do I have to, Daddy?"

"Yes, little mouse. Choose." Liam's big form was taking up the space in the doorway, his arms folded, watching Cammie closely. She went to the table and pulled open the drawer. She pulled out the paddle Liam had used on her the first night and set it down on the bed.

"One more," Liam prompted, and Cammie returned to the drawer. She knew which he preferred and pulled it out. It was a thick, silicone, vibrating dildo.

"Good girl, little mouse." Cammie had chosen to wear clothes that fit slightly looser in order to accommodate the diaper she had been made to wear. Cammie had only kept the diaper on because there was nowhere inconspicuous to discard it while she was removing the butt plug.

"Please take off your work clothes, Cammie," Liam asked, rolling up his sleeves and stepping into the room, closing the door behind him.

Our little girl has been very naughty. Liam texted Josie.

Naughty girls get punished. Make little Cammie understand. Josie texted back.

Liam set the phone aside and smiled; Cammie was standing in front of him, completely undressed except for the diaper.

"What do you want me to do, Daddy?"

Cammie asked, shivering slightly. Liam indicated the chair, and she immediately went to it, waiting for him to sit down.

Liam patted his lap, and Cammie bent over it, her hands resting on the carpet by his feet. Her legs were dangling on the other side, and her ass pointed into the air.

Using his bare hand, he brought it down onto her diapered ass, the sound loud because of the fabric. Cammie squirmed, but it wasn't from pain. Liam spanked her twice more, allowing the sound echo off the walls.

Liam undid the velcro sides of the diaper and folded the back of the diaper away. He could see for sure now that Cammie had removed her butt plug. Liam stroked her bottom slowly. Running his fingers over and down her ass, pressing a thumb to her ass hole, causing Cammie to shiver. He let his fingers continue their path, and he pressed a finger to her pussy lips, feeling her quiver beneath his touch.

Again Liam spanked her ass, this time without the protection of the diaper. Cammie squealed.

"Count."

And she did.

When they reached ten, he stopped and rubbed her ass again, "Stand."

Cammie obeyed, letting the diaper fall free. Without being prompted to, Cammie collected it and placed it on the bedside table.

"Good girl." Liam had the dildo in his hand, delighting in the way her eyes grew wider as she took notice of it in his possession. Cammie felt the heat pool between her legs. Liam's spanking had stirred the moisture to spread through her pussy, but seeing the hunger in his eyes, her heart thumped violently. Liam would never outright hurt her, but punishment was punishment, and the dildo was *huge*. She had never had it, or anything close to it, inside her.

"What do we say, Cammie?"

"I'm sorry, Daddy."

"Keep going."

"I'm sorry for taking my butt plug out and lying about it."

"Good, now," Liam pointed to the foot of the bed, and Cammie obeyed. She bent over the edge of the bed and spread her legs, now completely naked to his view.

"You seem to enjoy getting punished, little mouse."

"Yes, Daddy." Cammie hadn't attempted a lie this time, and Liam smiled.

"We're just getting started, Cammie. Lying is a very serious issue."

"Yes, Daddy." Cammie's hand went to her pussy lips, spreading them for Liam. Liam chuckled, "Not yet, little one." Liam placed the dildo in front of her. He wanted Cammie to see what he was about to put into her.

Liam fastened the fuzzy cuffs around her, ankles, "Are they comfortable? Do you remember your safe word?"

"Yes, Daddy." Cammie breathed.

Liam ran the head of the dildo over her pussy lips, letting her moisture coat it. It slid easily over her lips and her ass hole. Cammie stifled a small groan.

He pressed the tip of the dildo against her ass hole and pushed. Liam was careful as he slowly worked the head of the dildo into her hole. Cammie moaned, and her body instinctively stiffened, making Liam's effects harder.

"Relax, little one." Liam massaged the cheeks of her ass, spreading them further apart to ease the dildo in further. Cammie clawed at the bed coverings, dragging them closer. She bit into the folds and let out groans and small screams. Tears had gathered in the corners of her eyes, "Daddy, it's too much."

"You know what to do if you want me to stop, little mouse. You still have to be punished for lying to your Daddy."

Cammie sighed as a wave of pleasure hit her, making the tightness in her ass hole, bearable, "Yes, Daddy."

Liam worked the dildo in as far as it could go. Cammie was panting on the bed, and her pussy was coated in moisture from her pleasure. Her thighs glistened as well.

Liam's cock was as hard as ever, but he

maintained control as he touched her swollen clit with his finger. Cammie jerked, the sensation was startling and intense.

"I want to make sure, little mouse, that you never lie to your Daddy again."

"I won't lie again, Daddy, I promise." Cammie's voice was a rough whisper, and her hands were still fisted in the crumpled bedsheets.

"I want to make sure you don't lie to your Mommy again."

"I promise, Daddy, I promise." Cammie was bucking her hips as he massaged her clit.

"Let's make sure, little mouse." Liam pulled away, and Cammie whimpered. Liam grabbed the paddle from the bed and pressed it against Cammie's ass. Her entire body quivered.

"Count for Daddy, please, little mouse." Cammie counted, each followed by a hard *whack* from the paddle. Her bottom was burning, and Cammie whimpered for a different reason. When she reached five, Liam turned the vibrating function of the dildo on. Cammie arched her back and moaned loudly, "Daddy…" Cammie's voice was faint and broken by panting, but she continued to count for Liam. The blows were softer this time, making the vibration in her ass that much harder to ignore.

Liam set the paddle aside, watching the girl squirm and pant, clutching at the sheets, and biting into the fabric. Her ass hole was being stretched to its fullest by the thick dildo, juices flowing from both her holes.

"Daddy," Cammie half-growled as he switched the vibrator off. Her hand instantly went to her pussy, trying to ease the burn of desire.

"Cammie, stop," Liam ordered. Cammie pulled her hand away reluctantly, her pussy clenching and unclenching, causing more juices to flow from it.

"Good girl," Liam kissed the tender, red marks on her ass cheeks and wiggled the dildo, eliciting moans from Cammie as she pressed back against his hand.

"Wait here, little mouse. Don't touch."
Liam ordered and left the room.

Cammie lay panting, feeling the stretch of the dildo in her ass, feeling the thick girth of it as it filled her completely. It hurt still, but she was so close to an orgasm. She was tempted. She could just reach down…

Cammie stopped herself. Balling fistfuls of blanket in her hands to keep her from breaking more of the rules.

When Liam returned, Josie was with him, still dressed in her work uniform. She took up the empty chair and watched. Cammie was bound to the bed, her hair messed, and her face flushed. Josie saw the red marks on her bottom from where Liam had been punishing her.

Liam ran his hands over Cammie's ass cheeks again, heat coming off of them. He massaged them, pulling them apart and letting his hands trail down further. Liam stroked the outer lips of Cammie's pussy with his thumbs. His fingers were instantly coated, making them slip more readily into her folds.

Cammie moaned and caught Josie's eye. She was watching intently and unbuttoning the dark blue shirt of her uniform, only stopping to untie her hair. Cammie's pussy twitched.

Liam pushed his thumb deep into her pussy, feeling the heat and moisture, enjoying the way her muscles clamped onto him as her desire burned through her. Again, Liam pulled back, letting Cammie hover on the edge of her orgasm. The look in her eyes was wild, demanding, and her whimper was her plea.

Josie let her shirt fall away, and Cammie was afforded an excellent view of Josie's large breasts, enveloped in a lace bra that barely held onto the weight of them. Even from this distance, Cammie could tell that Josie's nipples were hard. She stood and unbuckled the belt of her pants, letting them slide down her thighs sensually. Liam started pumping the dildo in and out of Cammie's ass, causing her to groan in pleasure. A groan that ended in a growl when Liam stopped, "Daddy, please."

"Please, what, little mouse?" Liam asked

"Please don't stop, Daddy."

"Only good girls get to make demands, little Cammie," Josie said as she stepped out of her pants. Josie was still wearing her heeled boots. She looked intimidatingly beautiful, and Cammie stuffed another fistful of fabric in her mouth to stifle a moan.

Liam turned the vibrator back on and stepped towards Josie.

"Remember, little girl, no touching," Josie said as Liam pulled her to him and kissed her. It was hot and demanding, and Josie could feel his cock pressed against her, hard and throbbing. Her body responded to him instantly. Liam kissed her neck and slid his hands into her panties, stroking her. Josie threw her head back and sighed with pleasure, "Yes, Liam."

Liam inserted his fingers into her waiting pussy and stroked her slowly, licking her neck and breathing heavily into her ear. Josie moaned, and Cammie moaned in response to their play. Josie unzipped Liam's trousers and freed his cock. It was hard and throbbing and hot as she wrapped her hands around his shaft, stroking him as he fingered her. With Cammie watching them, her body tingled and burst into flame. Her pussy demanded his cock, but she knew Cammie's punishment would come first.

Cammie moaned again, bucking, trying to push the dildo deeper into her ass hole, attempting in vain to ease the ache in her pussy, "Mommy? Daddy? Please?"

Cammie was whimpering, and Liam's cock twitched again. "Go to her, Liam." Josie said breathlessly, "Show Cammie what happens to little girls who lie."

Liam kissed Josie, hard, pushing his fingers deeper into her wet hole, feeling her body clamp down as she came close to orgasming. He pulled away, a little reluctantly, and went to Cammie. Again, he stopped the vibrator, and the moan that escaped Cammie's lips was one of frustration and pure desire.

"Daddy," Cammie pushed herself up on her elbows, her pussy twitching and her body shivering from unspent need, "Daddy, please."

Liam knelt in front of Cammie, his cock at attention, thick, throbbing, and hot. Without asking for permission, Cammie wrapped her small fingers around his cock, her eyes dark with lust, and put her mouth around his head, flicking her tongue over it as Jose had demonstrated. Liam's eyes closed involuntarily, and a deep sigh of pleasure escaped his body, causing his cock to twitch violently and release beads of precum as his little girl continued pleasuring him. When Liam opened his eyes, he saw Josie standing behind Cammie, a grin on her face, "Our little girl is enjoying herself, Liam."

"She's soaked and dripping." Josie said, thickly, "Her pussy is twitching."
Liam groaned in response to Josie's words. She was making it harder for him to maintain control. He didn't want to cum yet.
Cammie opened her mouth wider and took his whole cock, slurping and massaging him with her tongue. She was a fast learner.

"You're getting good at that, little mouse." Liam's voice was hoarse, and Cammie moaned the second Josie touched the tip of her tongue to her swollen lips.

The vibration of Cammie's moan, combined with the view of his wife licking Cammie's pussy, was nearly enough to make him lose control. He pulled away, shaking. Liam met Josie's gaze and saw the mischief in her eyes. She knew how to push him. Cammie moaned again as Josie slipped a finger into her pussy, stroking her. Liam sank to his knees in front of Josie and spread her legs. As Josie adjusted for Liam, she pushed another finger into Cammie's soaking pussy. Then another. The girl's entire body quivered, right on the edge of her orgasm. Josie pulled away, again denying Cammie release.

"Promise us, Cammie, that you will never lie again. No matter what."

"I promise, Mommy." Liam's tongue slid between Josie's pussy lips, and a moan escaped. Cammie repeated herself, again and again. She meant it, and with every word, Cammie seemed to be struggling to control her tears, "From the bottom of my heart, Mommy. I promise."

"Good girl, Cammie." With that, Josie wiggled the dildo, then proceeded to fuck her small hole with the large object. Cammie moaned, louder than before, and pushed back against Josie's hands as her fingers found her wet pussy again.

Cammie's body was flushed, glistening with pleasure and sweat. She couldn't take the torment any longer. She pushed back against Josie's hands, attempting to increase the pressure that Josie was exerting. It was no use. Josie pulled away again, and Cammie was left panting, crying, and pleading.

Josie could feel her own body twitch and convulse as she came closer and closer to that edge. She could understand the complete madness that Cammie felt as her orgasm kept being denied. Liam pulled away from Josie, and she immediately went to Cammie's other side. Josie lay in front of Cammie and spread her legs open for the girl, baring herself to her. Josie was wet from her own juices and Liam's tongue. Cammie stared and licked her lips, "Can I touch you, Mommy?”

"Yes, sweet girl."

Cammie gingerly ran her finger through the folds of Josie's pussy. Her skin was soft, and the juices were sticky. Her scent was driving Cammie mad, so she pressed her lips to Josie's pussy and pushed her tongue into her hole.

Josie rested her head back as Cammie's tongue lapped at her clit, then circled it, varying the pressure, "Good girl, Cammie."

Liam pressed his cock against Cammie's waiting pussy, it twitched. He gripped his cock in his fist and ran it across her wet lips, coating it as he had done with the dildo. It took less time than it did before.

From his vantage point, Liam could see Josie's pussy on display for their little girl. She was obediently licking and sucking on Josie's clit, her body responding to the scent and taste of her Mommy by becoming wetter, and her hips grinding in the air, begging for release. Cammie pushed back against Liam's cock.

As a matter to get himself under control so he

wouldn't cum the second he entered her, Liam stroked her pussy with the head of his cock and pumped the dildo in and out of her ass. It was still there, filling Cammie's small hole, stretching it as far as it could go. Cammie had gotten used to it and was pushing back in time with his play. Both Josie and Cammie moaned in unison. Josie, from Cammie's continuous suckling, and Cammie from Liam's play.

Liam's cock burned with need. He felt his desire build up in his belly. Slowly, Liam pushed his cock into Cammie's waiting pussy. It gripped his cock tightly, twitching and clamping down on him as he entered her. The dildo in her ass was taking up enough space that he could feel it pressing against his own cock as he slowly slid in and out of Cammie's pussy.

The girl moaned, then whimpered, "Yes, Daddy, please, fuck me." Instead of scolding her, Liam thrust his cock balls deep into her. He wanted Cammie to feel his every thrust as he entered her; he wanted the girl to understand that punishment and reward could be doled out as he saw fit. Cammie had inserted her entire hand into Josie's pussy, pushing her fist in and out of her, causing thick globs of sticky fluid to smear over her arm and drip onto the bed.

Josie's moans were becoming louder, and Cammie's body was responding to them.

Liam gripped Cammie's hips and pulled out just far enough that just the head of his cock remained inside of her. Even with the large amount of lubrication, the girl's pussy was so tight that it took effort not to pound her into sweet oblivion.

"Cammie?"

"Yes, Daddy?" She was breathless and shaking.

"Do you want to cum?"

"Yes, please, Daddy. Make me cum."

Josie's own scream of pleasure caused Cammie's pussy to twitch a few times. "Please, Daddy," she repeated again, a crack in her voice.

Liam leaned over her, still only keeping the head of his cock in her hole, "Alright, little mouse. Ask me again, and mean it."

"Please," Cammie whimpered, her voice was thick, and she begged Liam, "Please, please make me cum, Daddy."

"Again." Liam thrust in slowly, feeling her pussy contract around him.

"Make me cum on your cock, Daddy. Pretty please, Daddy. I need to cum." Cammie's pleas were sweet and satisfying as he increased his speed. Cammie no longer bothered muffling her moans and screams. He pounded his cock into Cammie, pushing harder and stroking faster. Liam gripped her hips tightly and thrust into her, feeling his orgasm peak just as she screamed her final release.

Cammie's body twitched and convulsed around his cock, drawing him closer to the edge before her second orgasm ripped through her. Her small body clenched so hard he gave a guttural growl as his cock shot ropes of cum into her pussy, over and over again.

Cammie's breaths came in gasps. Her body was shaking and shivering, convulsing around his cock, slowly causing the dildo to push itself out.

Liam switched it on and held it in place. The vibrations shot through her, causing her to scream once more. Cammie's body clamped down on his cock, hard, and he groaned from the pleasure of it.

When Liam's cock stopped twitching, he slipped it out of Cammie's filled pussy, watching as cum dripped out, running down her thighs and onto the bed.

Liam's cock was still hard, and he stroked it slowly, coating his hand in their juices. He felt a second orgasm building, and he pumped his cock hard and fast, shooting more cum over Cammie's ass and back.

Liam stood panting, enjoying the view that lay before him. Cammie was covered in his cum and her own fluids. The vibrator was still sticking out of her ass, causing Cammie to moan continuously, thrashing her head from side to side. Josie lay in front of Cammie, the girl's fist still inside Josie's pussy. By the look on Josie's face, Cammie was clenching and unclenching her fists. Cammie's trembling was causing her a great deal of pleasure.

Cammie let out a long, deep moan as Liam slowly pulled the dildo free from her ass. With a sigh, the girl collapsed, her body trembling.

"Cammie," Josie called, "one more time, little one. Please make Mommy cum." Cammie obeyed, her hair damp and her body glittering from their play. Her fist was still inside Josie's pussy, and soon Cammie's tongue was working on her clit.

Liam left the two on the bed, and he snuck out of the room for a shower.

Chapter 11

Cammie had been awaiting this day for the last thirty days, and it was about time it got here. While she had grown to enjoy some things about her community service, it was certainly not something she wanted to keep doing. She was grateful that her sentence had been light.

Today also marked her thirty days sober. She had attended the court-mandated meetings and had found that she genuinely benefited from them and decided that she would continue the meetings.

The agency assured her that the hours and everything else required by the court would be handed over properly.

Cammie found that the time spent serving the community sometimes allowed her to learn new things about herself. As an example, Cammie knew that she *hated* cooking. She had spent time both serving the food as well as making it at the soup kitchen she was assigned to. It was too much stress. What she did love, however, was talking with the old people at the retirement village. Cammie intended to continue helping out even after her service ended.

As usual, Liam had offered to drive Cammie wherever she needed to go. Cammie had managed to get her car from the police impound lot a week ago but had fallen into a relaxed kind of routine with them.

Today, however, Cammie had asked Liam if she could drive herself.

"I thought you liked it when I drove you around, little mouse."

"I do, Daddy," Cammie giggled, "but I think I should at least drive myself on my last day." When Liam just looked at her, Cammie continued, "So I can show you and Mommy that I've learned my lesson."

"Have you learned your lesson, Cammie?"

"Yes, Daddy." Cammie had such a serious look on her face that Liam could not help but chuckle.

"If you are sure, little mouse."
Cammie nodded enthusiastically, smiling broadly.

Cammie greeted the people she had come to know over the last thirty days warmly. They were all celebrating their last day today, which meant the atmosphere was supercharged with excitement and joy.
The last day was also the hardest that their supervisor had scheduled. It was nearly a hundred degrees out today. They were working the last quarter-mile stretch on the road out of town, so not too many cars came through this early in the day. Still, even in the sweltering heat, their morale did not falter.
They joked, laughed, danced, and miraculously, worked faster than they had in any previous assignment on this particular stretch of road. Weeds were pulled up, trash was collected, and sharp objects disposed of.
Cammie was cheerful, even as sweat ran down her back and into the diaper she was still

wearing. It was mildly uncomfortable, but Liam had promised that if she continued being a good girl, she got to take it off and only wear it at night.

Cammie had all but skipped to her car that afternoon, her heart lighter than it had been since the month had started. Her first stop was Liam and Josie's home.

My home, too. Cammie corrected. Cammie loved living with them. She was happier and healthier than she had ever been in her life.

Cammie stripped out of her overalls that they had bought specifically for the community service. It had made her feel more secure that no one could see her diaper when she wore the overalls.

Cammie stuffed her dirty clothes in the hamper and discarded the sweaty diaper in the bin next to it. She ran to the shower naked, giggling as she went. She was home alone but still felt giddy at the thought of being caught naked.

She washed the heat of the day from her body, loving the way the water flowed over her. The soft caress reminded her of Liam and Josie's touches, and her body tingled in response.

Cammie wanted to touch herself but held off. She was better at following the rules, now, too. She dried off, replaced the diaper, and got dressed.

The real reason for Cammie wanting to drive herself was that she wanted to get Liam and Josie a few small things to say thank you.

At the start of all of this, she had acted like a complete brat. *More than what was called for, to be sure,* Cammie thought. They had taught her that there was more than one way to deal with messy emotions.

Not only that, but Liam and Josie had also taken her in and cared for her. Despite her nearly losing her job and her apartment. Cammie had managed to get through her near-miss relatively unscathed.

***

"Mommy? Daddy?" Cammie began.

Liam and Josie sat side by side on the couch and waited. Cammie had texted them and asked them to meet her in the living room as soon as they got home.

"I want to say something, and it's very important."

"Go on, little mouse." Liam encouraged.

"When we met, I was-" Cammie paused to try to find the words, "everything was a big mess." Cammie knelt in front of them and took both Liam and Josie's hands into her own and held on to them.

"You taught me that messes can be cleaned up."
Liam and Josie exchanged a look and then looked back at Cammie.

"What is this about, sweetheart?" Josie asked, rubbing her thumb over the back of Cammie's hand wrapped around hers. Cammie's face flushed, but she didn't waver, "I got you guys something today."

"Is that why you were so secretive this morning?" Liam asked, a frown wrinkling his forehead.

Cammie nodded, her face turning redder, "I wanted it to be a surprise."

"Alright, alright! Don't keep us waiting." Josie laughed and shooed Cammie.

A short minute later, Cammie returned, struggling with a big gift bag.

Liam got up and offered her a hand, to which Cammie stuck her tongue out at, "No, I can do this, Daddy."

Liam chuckled and returned to his seat, "Alright, little mouse, we can do this your way."

Cammie, satisfied, plopped the bag down in front of them and reached inside.

"This one is for Daddy," she said and handed him a carefully wrapped object. "And this one is for Mommy," Cammie said and handed her a similar looking package. Liam opened his and stared at it. It must have been the biggest mug he had ever seen. He turned it over.

"Best Daddy in the world?" Liam's voice had a hint of laughter, but he managed to suppress it, "I love it, little mouse."

Josie unwrapped hers, and it had the same basic sentiment on it.

Cammie looked excitedly at Josie, "They also change color when you add hot water."

Josie stood and dutifully turned the kettle on and waited for it to boil. She poured the water into the mug and watched as the black mug turned white.

Josie's eyes grew wider in surprise, "Cammie!" Cammie giggled.

"What is it, Jo?" Liam asked, an amused smile still on his lips.

Josie returned to her seat to show them. Instead of "Best Mommy in the World," a large, pink pussy replaced it.

Liam's eyes flickered to the bag, "Did you go to the naughty store?"

Cammie's eyes glittered, and her face turned a shade redder, "Maybe."

Cammie pulled out a large wooden paddle and handed it to her Daddy.

When the gifts had been doled out, Cammie threw her arms around Josie, "I promise I won't be that bad ever again, Mommy."

"I have one more present," Cammie said as she stood and unbuttoned her blouse. She didn't take it off yet, wanting to make a show of it. The lady at the store had helped her get into it. Cammie unbuttoned her jeans and very slowly slid it down her lean legs and kicked it off. The blouse afforded enough cover that only the barest of hints of flesh was shown. Cammie hadn't asked for permission to go without her diaper, but she had had to make a choice. The harness and diaper wouldn't both fit under her clothes, and the diaper would ruin the visual she was going for, so she had removed it.

There was one more thing that she had gotten for herself while she was out shopping. As her jeans slid down, a furry tail popped free. Cammie bit her lower lip as Liam and Josie looked on in awe. Cammie turned around and wiggled her bottom at them, her blouse covering most of her ass, but the tail hanging freely.

She heard Liam suck in a breath, and her body started tingling. She expected that she would be punished for not wearing the diaper, but for now, Cammie was basking in the rapt attention from Liam and Josie.

Cammie turned to face them. She was shaking a little, her nerves were on fire, and her body tingled and burned in response.

Then she made a show of walking to the bag and pulling out the matching headpiece that came with the tail. Cammie bent low, exposing her ass to Liam and Josie. The tail was blocking a full view of her already moist pussy lips, but the effect was what she had intended.

Cammie's heart was racing as she turned her back on them again. Liam and Josie were quiet but had not once taken their eyes off of her. Cammie was mesmerizing.

"Are you guys ready?" Cammie asked innocently.

"Ready for?" Josie asked, her eyes still looking at the way the tail swayed back and forth as Cammie moved.

"Your final present," Cammie said and lifted the hem of her blouse, revealing the straps of the gray leather harness. The leather was tight against her skin, and the buckles hot from her body heat. Cammie lowered the blouse from her shoulders, slowly inching it down, exposing her back. There were no straps there, just bare, silky flesh that glowed under the bright lights.

"There was just one more way I could show you how much you mean to me," Cammie said, "Only one way to show how happy my Mommy and Daddy have made me." Cammie dropped the blouse to the ground, completely naked now except for the harness. Cammie wiggled her ass again, making the tail wiggle back and forth. She dropped to her knees and looked over her shoulder at them. Cammie grabbed the end of the tail in her hand and stuck the end of it in her mouth, suckling on it. Josie saw that the tail was a butt plug and not attached to the harness. Josie licked her lips, and Liam cleared his throat, "Cammie."

"I want you and Mommy to teach me how to be naughty." Cammie looked at them, her eyes dark, and spread her legs a little, exposing her most sensitive parts to the air and light. A shiver ran down her spine.

"Little mouse," Liam started but couldn't quite tell her no.

"Please, Daddy?" Cammie stretched her arms out in front of her, arching her back. Cammie rose to her feet slowly and faced them. The harness was tied around her throat, and straps ran down the front of her, between her breasts and tight against her skin. The straps of the harness came together at her hips, where another strap encircled them. More straps ran from her hips down to her thighs. There were metal loops for ropes, clips, and other straps. Something Cammie had insisted upon.

"Do you like it?" Cammie asked, uncertain, as she twirled around for them again.

"I love it, little mouse, Liam said.

"Did you pick it out yourself?" Josie asked and circled Cammie.

"I did, Mommy. I thought of what you might like, and the lady helped me."

Cammie swayed her hips, swinging the end of the tail in her hands and made herself comfortable on Josie's lap. Josie was stunned. Their meek little mouse had turned slightly wild.

"Please, Mommy? I really want to show you that I have learned my lesson." Cammie nuzzled Josie's neck, planting soft kisses along her jaw and behind her ear.

Josie pressed herself against Cammie's back, feeling her heat seep through her clothes, "Well, then, little one, we should put it to good use." Cammie jumped in surprise as Josie's fingers touched her moist pussy lips, and she threw her head back against Josie's shoulder. Josie expertly drew moans from Cammie's lips as Liam watched.

"What happens when you break the rules, little mouse?"

"I get punished."

"That's right."

"What happens if you are a good girl?" With that, Josie pulled her hand away, and Cammie knew she wasn't about to have her way just yet.

"On your knees, little girl," Josie demanded. Cammie obeyed instantly, her eyes glossing over just a little as she felt the tail being tugged as she dropped to her knees. Josie had the tip in her hands and was rhythmically tugging on it. The sensation rippled through Cammie, and her pussy twitched.
Liam approached her, a leather leash in his hands. The one that came with the harness. He clipped the leash to the metal ring at her neck and pulled the slack tight.

"Daddy?"

"Yes, little mouse?"

"Are you mad at me? I only wanted to do something special for you." Cammie's voice was soft, and her eyes were staring up at him, trusting and a little scared.

"No, little one. We're not angry." Josie said and stroked her hair.

"Mommy's right," Liam said, smiling down at her, "but you know the rules, little mouse. You weren't allowed to take your diaper off until we got home.”

“I know, Daddy.”

Liam dropped to his knees in front of her, pulling her face up to his and kissed the tip of her nose, “Your punishment will be over before you even know it.”

“Okay, Daddy.” Cammie smiled, relieved.

“Good girl.”

“Now, open your mouth, little mouse,” Liam commanded as he unzipped his pants. Cammie licked her lips, unable to hide her desire and did as she was told.

The leather leash was pulled tighter, forcing Cammie closer to his hard cock. Cammie gripped his cock and held it steady, slowly running her tongue around the swollen head.

“No, Cammie, no teasing.”

Cammie stopped and opened her mouth wide. Liam thrust his throbbing cock into her waiting mouth and pulled the leash tighter. There was very little for Cammie to do except take his cock as deep as she could. Cammie sucked his cock into her throat, feeling it fill her up. She gagged, and Liam pulled out slightly, giving her a moment to breathe. She nodded, and Liam pushed deeper, feeling his hardness slide deep into her throat. Cammie knew she had to relax, or she would choke again. Tears were forming in the corners of her eyes as Liam thrust a slow rhythm.

Josie joined Cammie on the floor, running her hands over Cammie's body, pinching her nipples and delighting in the muffled moans coming from her. Josie reached around and ran her fingers through Cammie's pussy lips, coating her fingers in her moisture.

Josie licked her lips and looked up at Liam, her eyes meeting his. There was a lot of heat and desire in them, but also love.

"Cammie," Josie whispered in her ear, flicking a fingertip over Cammie's nipple. Cammie whined softly, unable to respond verbally. Josie increased her strokes in Cammie's pussy, feeling her body clutch at her fingers as her pleasure built.

"Cum for Mommy, little girl," Josie

commanded.

Liam thrust his cock deep into Cammie's throat, watching as the girl's body shivered and twitched under Josie's intense touch. Cammie's body clenched around Josie's fingers, begging for more. Cammie swallowed his cock as far as it could go, feeling his hardness twitch as she did so. Her orgasm flooded through her, eliciting deep moans of pleasure.

Liam groaned loudly as he orgasmed, cum filling up Cammie's little mouth. He pulled back slightly and let some slack out of the leash, cum leaking from the corners of her mouth.

When his cock stopped twitching, and he pulled out of her mouth. Cammie continued licking and cleaning cum from his cock, suckling and enjoying the grunts she could draw from him with that small act.

"Good girl, little mouse."

Cammie panted, moans filling the room, and leaned back into Josie's warm body, her fingers drawing Cammie's orgasm out. She twitched and shivered.

"Do you want more, little girl?"

"Yes, Mommy," Cammie whispered, delirious.

"What do we say?"

"Please, Mommy."

"That's a good girl," Josie said and pinched Cammie's nipple, hard. Cammie moaned louder, pressing herself against Josie as her fingers continued teasing her nipples and her pussy.

"Jo, let's give this good little girl the treat she wants," Liam said and pulled on the leash. Cammie reluctantly pulled away from Josie's teasing touch and stood. Cammie's legs were slightly unsteady as she walked behind Liam, led by the leash to Liam and Josie's room.

We Will Never Leave You, Baby Girl

An MDLG and DDLG story about Alice, an ABDL little who completed her Mommy and Daddy's lives

Tina Moore

Chapter 1

"When are you going to grow up?" His words struck her like a punch to the gut, followed closely by a wave of white-hot anger. He had known exactly where to target his words - precisely known how to bait her. Alice had walked right into it. She had shown her vulnerability to him. She had opened up, and that had proven to be a massive error in judgment time and time again.

Alice ran her hands through her dark hair, scraping her scalp with her fingernails. She gripped fistfuls of it and held it there, tightening her grip as she fought to restrain herself from physically assaulting him. She sighed and dropped her hands again. Alice had tried to explain it to him a few times before, but he didn't seem quite to understand. Or he didn't *want* to understand. She could feel tears well up and sting her eyes. No way was she going to allow him to make her cry again, not this time. She had given him so many chances, but David couldn't see past her freakish childish behavior (his words, not hers). She wasn't a freak. She just liked being taken care of. She *needed* to be taken care of.

"You're a grown-ass adult. It's time to act like it. I'm not here to take care of some bratty bitch," his words cut through her thoughts, setting her resolve.

"Nice," Alice said dryly.

"What? It's fucking true," David shouted. They stared at each other for half a second in tense, angry silence before she took a deep breath.

"Fine," Alice plainly said.

"What?" David questioned, annoyed, and wanting to hurt her.

"I'm done," Alice clenched her jaw and shut down her emotions. That was her go-to. She would deal with the fallout later. Right now, she was fighting it so she could get herself out of there.

"What are you talking about?" David aggressively questioned.

"I'm leaving, David," Alice softly replied.

"You can't just leave in the middle of a fight, Alice!" The furry in his eyes made Alice's stomach churn.

"Watch me," Alice said, snatching her keys off of the coffee table and stomping to the door as he threw every name in the book at her. She let his words wash over her but kept her composure as best she could.

"You'll never be happy, Alice, because no one will want you. *Ever*," David had driven the final blade as deep as he could. Alice knew it was because his ego had been hurt, but she couldn't let this one slide. She wheeled to face him, the door open with her hand grasping the knob, "Excuse me?"

"You're broken. You can't function alone, and you know it," David remarked, impressed with the pain he was causing her. The color drained from her face. David's smirk twisted the knife in her gut, "You're stuck in your messed-up past." Alice could feel her anger flash through her. It threatened to form her hand into a fist at the end of her arm as she slammed the door behind her. She took the stairs down as fast as she could, placing as much distance between them before she did something stupid like punching him in his obnoxious face.

She sat in the driver's seat of her car. She was shaking, holding on to her tenuous emotions that were roiling around inside of her like white rapids. She knew David was less than accommodating to her lifestyle, as he had put it, but Alice had thought that he would be able to get over it. She had thought that he would eventually just get used to Alice retreating into her little space on occasion. He had even seemed into it the first few times. When aftercare was required, he had mysteriously remembered that he had some errand to run. Eventually, he had stopped coming up with excuses and simply refused. She should have gotten out then, but of course, Alice had stubbornly held out with a vague hope that he would change.
David had known which buttons to push to make

her hurt because she had given him the ammunition and painted a giant target on her back. They had been together for a year - one long, unsatisfying, stressful year, and she had let him in.

It amazed her that she had stayed with him for so long. At that moment, Alice knew that she had never intended to be with him for the amount of time that she had. She had only stayed with him out of—what? Desperation? Loneliness? Alice clenched her teeth, jammed the key in the ignition, and tore out of the parking lot. If only she could run away from her thoughts and feelings as quickly as she could escape David. Alice hated that she couldn't stand to be alone. She hated that David could even remotely be right.

By the time Alice pulled her small, dinged-up car into the parking lot of her less-than-ideal apartment block, tears had already drawn black streaks down her cheeks. Smudges made worse by her wiping at the tears as they fell. It was late in the afternoon on a Friday. Alice sat in her car, watching the neighborhood kids running around, laughing, utterly oblivious to the world around them. Alice wanted to be just as carefree, just as—just as happy, she decided. But whenever she exposed her little side, she had the wind knocked out of her. First Vi, then Danielle, and now David. Alice couldn't' blame them. She hadn't been exactly open with them about her needs. She closed her eyes and took a deep, steadying breath. Her tears were still running down her face. There was no stopping the dam from breaking anymore, and it was only a matter of time before she knew her phone would ping non-stop. She knew without looking that it would be David. Every fight that had ended in Alice leaving his place resulted in his angry, pleading, and often crazy messages.

Alice wiped at another stray tear and finally made her way to her apartment, kicking the car door shut with her boot and shrugging her purse over her shoulder.

It was small, but it was home, and it was hers.

Alice had painstakingly cleaned every scuff mark, scrubbed the carpet within an inch of fraying the fibers. It was clean, tidy, and it always smelled sweet and fruity.

Her phone pinged again as she dumped her stuff on the kitchen counter.

"Oh my God," Alice growled, gritting her teeth, "Will you leave me alone?" She opened the messages, reading through each one.

Babe, I'm sorry

Let's talk

You're a bitch

I don't know why I said that. I'll try to get better at this

Give me another chance

Ping. The screen scrolled up as each new message filled the page with black lines.

You'll come back, I know it. You just can't stay away

Ping.

Fuck you, Alice

Ping. Frustrated and angry, Alice threw herself and her phone onto her bed facedown, stifling a groan with the bundle of messy bedsheets balled in her fists. Her moan slowly turned into another sob that got stuck in her throat. She turned her head sideways and allowed her mouth room to breathe.

It would be easy to go back. It would be so simple just to pick up where they left off. She had done it before.

"Fuck him," Alice said to herself.

She pushed herself up, grabbed everything that was scattered around, and shoved all of it into the washing hamper. After a minute, she realized that some of David's clothes had ended up in there as well. She hastily pulled those pieces out, sending shirts and boxers flying everywhere. She swore again, angrily picking up pieces of clothing and trying to avoid letting David's stuff touch hers.

Alice sat down on the floor in defeat, burying her hands in her hair with her head on her knees. She had invited David over a couple of times throughout their relationship, but he rarely stayed the night.

"I don't like the kid stuff," he had
commented off-handedly, pulling his boots back
on after she had given him what he wanted. The
feelings of abandonment had welled up in her
again, as David waltzed out of her apartment.
She had gone to his place the next morning
seeking comfort, and they had fallen in bed
together again. It never went further than that.
Bringing it up only made him angry, and their
relationship was new, so she felt vulnerable.
He didn't care for the aftercare portion of their
activities, and eventually, Alice had stopped
pushing. Enough time had passed that she'd kept
that part of herself hidden as far away from him
as possible, only rarely breaking. Yet still, she
had gotten rapped over the knuckles.
Alice allowed the tears to flow, and the sobbing
sounds to tear from her throat. They came from
deep within her, drawing upon the loneliness she
felt. It wasn't like she missed him—not really.
But she didn't like being alone, and now that
David was out of her life, the reminder that she
had no one had come crashing home, the force

strong enough to break her.

The weight of her emotions threatened to crush her as Alice lay down, curling in on herself on the thinly carpeted floor. She stuffed fistfuls of duvet into her mouth to stifle her wails. The dam had been broken.

Eventually, the tears stopped falling, and her sobs drained out of her, transforming into light hiccoughs. She remained in her curled position, with her head against her knees for a while longer, feeling the hollowness left behind by the anger and sorrow. She tilted her head so she could glance around the room, darkness having invaded in the absence of light.

She inhaled shakily and pushed herself into a seated position again. Alice stared at the closet doors, unblinking as she struggled with her mind telling her to leave it be. Alice wanted to get rid of everything that made her different, but she shoved that thought away.

There wasn't space in her already overfilled, overstressed brain to feel weird about her kink. She sighed, wiped at her eyes, and methodically started cleaning up her scattered life. Every so often, Alice would burst into tears again as she remembered David's words assaulted her. They had been what Alice was already thinking, and it rubbed her the wrong way that he could be right. She pulled herself together and finally cleaned the rest of her small apartment, tossing David's things into a garbage bag and leaving it by the front door. Alice pulled the sheets off her bed and stuffed everything else into the hamper along with it.

When she was satisfied with the bareness of her room, she went to the small bathroom that was hidden by a closet door. The design had struck Alice as odd, but she had gotten used to it over the years. She assumed that owners of the apartment block had intended to save money by breaking into a small storage room through her closet instead of ripping the whole wall out to remodel the old building.

She sat on the edge of the bath, popped the plug into the hole, and turned on the water. Alice poured a very generous dollop of sweetpeascented bubble bath into the running stream. She wiped at the moisture on her face and watched the bubbles grow and foam as the warm water filled the tub. She dropped a small bright orange bath bomb in the water and deeply inhaled the sweet citrus scent as it fizzed and bobbed, turning the water orange. She smiled as the glitter swirled through the bubbles. Alice turned the water off and stripped herself of her clothes, kicking them into a pile in the corner of the bathroom. She would deal with that later. She brushed her hands through her dark hair and pouted at the puffy-eyed reflection of herself as the bathroom filled with steam and the scent of blossoms and soapy bubbles. She carefully removed her industrial and her septum piercings and set them into the cup sitting on the sink. Alice smiled at her reflection, then shook her head. She pulled a face, baring her teeth at herself. She giggled and poured a little cleaning solution into the cup. She dampened a clump of cotton wool and washed the tiny pinpricks where she had just removed the piercings.

Alice smiled again at her reflection, feeling her body relax slowly. She carefully washed her face, getting rid of the smeared streaks of mascara. Her dark, deep red lipstick followed the same fate. She admired herself for a moment, her big, green, cat-like eyes looking back at her. She might not have been classically beautiful, but she had that edgy beauty that captivated people. Alice happily hummed as she half-danced, half-wiggled in place as she pulled her long hair up into a knot. The bright pink under-color was finally exposed. Alice grinned and stuffed her hair into a flowery shower cap. She walked naked to her portable speaker and plugged her phone into the jack. She hit shuffle and danced her way back to the bathroom as her favorite songs filled the apartment.

She tested the water, goosebumps spreading over her exposed skin. She slid into the warmth and delighted in the way the remaining bath bomb fizzed between her toes. Alice laughed as she slid unexpectedly a little deeper beneath the water in the slippery tub and sighed happily. Alice scooped a palm-full of bubbles and blew them into the air, watching the tiniest ones swirl and fall slowly back down. She allowed her body to sink even deeper beneath the water until the bubbles tickled her nose. Alice blew hard into the foam covering her lips and giggled at the small spray as the foam exploded outward.

She spent enough time in the bath to turn her fingers wrinkly and the water uncomfortably cold. Alice wrapped herself in a soft, fluffy towel, rubbing the fabric over her skin. She could feel some tears welling up again, but took a few deep, steadying breaths and forced those emotions away. She liked being who she was, and she wasn't going to let an ass like David bully her into changing.

She walked back to her room and dug through the box of things in the back of her closet and found her favorite blankie. Alice also pulled her stuffed giant koala out of the box.

"Beanie!" She exclaimed, delighted, snuggling him close to her breast. He was nearly half her size and incredibly soft. She'd gotten

Beanie on a whim when she had first moved in.
Alice felt a tug from deep inside of her, a
comforting safety that allowed her to sink into
the warmth of his curly fur completely. Alice
closed her eyes and held him for a moment.
Inside was a bunch of her little clothes, ribbons,
and coloring things. Alice tucked Beanie onto her
lap as she rummaged through the box, carefully
unpacking everything she had hidden from
David. She pulled her paci out and went to rinse
it off in the sink before putting it in her mouth.
She had come across tubes of paint and laughed
as she squeezed a blob onto her finger and
smeared it across the edge of the box. She did the
same thing with each of the colors and drew an
abstract picture that vaguely looked like a fat,
rainbow-colored penguin.

She felt her whole body unwinding, releasing the
tension she had been holding in. Alice tried to
wipe away as much of the paint as possible on
the box, letting the rest dry as she hummed.
She stroked Beanie's fur and hummed to herself.
She lay down on her stomach, still hugging

Beanie tightly beneath one arm. Alice had taken out one of her favorite coloring books and turned to a random page. On it was a beach scene with a couple of puppies, a giant beach ball, and a crumpled, sand-covered blanket. Alice poured the box of wax crayons out on the bedroom floor and carefully chose the perfect color for the beach blanket.

She was halfway through when she decided to color one of the dogs a bright pink and wrote *Strawbs* as small as possible in the space that was meant to be the collar.

Without realizing it, Alice had begun drifting off to sleep. The week had been long and hard, and the drama of the day had drained her of the rest of her energy.

Alice startled awake, the light still on, crayon in hand. She yawned, dropped the crayon, and crawled into her bed with Beanie held close.

***

Alice woke, her dark hair messy, and her eyes

were struggling to open in the late morning light. She had stayed up long past her usual bedtime, making a mess of her room as she dug through the boxes of things she had hidden in the back of her closet.

She spent the rest of the morning and most of the afternoon in bed, scrolling through YouTube and Instagram, looking at how her favorite creators repainted old dolls and made them new clothes. Alice loved watching them get their tiny makeovers, from their fresh faces to the brand new hairstyles and their teeny-tiny outfits. The dolls were pre-loved, their hair knotted and dirty, and their plastic faces smeared with muck and some form of colored marker.

It reminded her that no matter how messed up something might be. It could still be made beautiful.

Alice snuggled Beanie and pressed play on the next video. She didn't want to get up yet, even though she knew she had to send out her resume if she wanted to find something that paid better. Alice had fallen asleep again, waking up when

the sun had already dipped below the horizon.
Her stomach growled unhappily, and she rolled
out of bed, logging into a delivery app for dinner.
She spent the rest of the night eating Chinese
takeout and scrolling through Instagram.

Early on Sunday morning, Alice woke feeling less
fragile and took a quick shower.
She organized her room and threw the empty
box in the trash. She wouldn't have to hide her
little things anymore. She smiled at that thought,
happiness blooming inside of her. She carefully
fixed up her resume, changing details, and
adding in others where appropriate. She spent
the better part of the day, sending it out to
potential employers and recruiting agencies.
While Alice enjoyed her current job, the amount
of time she spent doing nothing was slowly
driving her insane. She brought coffee and
occasionally filed a document. Her office
manager had a habit of micromanaging and
eventually just took over every task himself. Alice
had learned to shrug it off, but it was beginning

to get on her nerves.

She had worked nearly as many jobs as there were weeks in the year, and each one had given her one thing or another to complain about. It was just the way things were. If it wasn't horrible hours, it was a ridiculous workload. However, she knew that despite the experience and *potential* for growth in her current position promised. She needed stability and better pay. That is why she had applied just about everywhere, taking the time to write a cover letter for each company and position. When she had quit her first sales job for better prospects, Alice had been nervous and felt guilty. They had, after all, given her a chance to prove herself, and they had also offered to allow her to finish her schooling through them. Her boss pulled her aside and wished her the best of luck, reminding her, "Don't look for something you know; look for somewhere you can grow."

***

On Tuesday and Wednesday nights, Alice worked a shift at her local mom-and-pop pizza place. It wasn't glamorous, but it paid well in tips, especially since the clientele had come to know and recognize her. She had worked for the owners since she was sixteen, taking it as a second and often third job. She busted her ass and took as many shifts as she could safely handle, but often pushed herself to the point of exhaustion.

Alice had come home in the very early hours of the morning, the air chilly and her breath making small puffs of cloud as she exhaled. The local pizza place was one of the very last to stay open, often drawing in customers from many walks of life. Her favorite, of course, was the stoner college kid crowd that had the munchies and often hilarious and disastrous stories to share regarding their smoking experiences. This usually meant that she only closed shop well after midnight. Alice also helped clean up and prep dough for the next day's business. It was tough work, but Alice had grown to like how busy she was while running the ovens.

"Alice."

Alice looked up from her hands, where she was fumbling with her keys. David's sudden appearance caused her to jump.

"What are you doing here, David?" Alice asked angrily, masking her sudden unease and the flood of desire. For all his faults, the man was good looking. His light hair was sticking out beneath his cap. His dark, smoldering eyes pierced her.

"We aren't done," he said, stepping towards her, gripping her arm tightly.

"Yeah, we are. Leave," Alice said, shrugging him off as she pushed past him to her door. Her body was tense, and she made a show of shoving her key in the lock, waiting for his departure.

"No, you threw a childish tantrum and left," David replied.

"You are not giving me any reason to stay with you right now, David," Alice said as she rolled her eyes, masking her fear as best she could, but her heart hammering. Would her neighbors hear her if she screamed?

"Come on, Alice. You and I both know you're going to come back to me anyway. Why not just do it sooner rather than later?" David said, his voice soothing and apologetic, coaxing and tugging at her desire to be wanted.

"David—" Alice started but then stopped herself.

"Baby, please. I'm sorry," David gently stroked his hand over her arm, and she stared at it.

Alice turned to him, "You're not here to make up. You're here for a booty call." Alice inhaled deeply through her nose, unable to quite process what was happening.

"Are you *kidding* me?" She said, fresh anger coursing through her veins.

David shrugged.

"Is that so bad? I mean, we were great together." She stared at him, horrorstruck. She turned the knob, kicking the door open, and grabbed his stuff, tossing the garbage bag at him.

"David, we're done. Go home," Alice turned around and swiftly slammed and locked the door behind her. She leaned her back against it, listening. She expected him to start hammering on her door, but it never came.

***

It was already late in the evening the following Friday when her phone's notification bell rang and startled her.

She sighed, dropping her head to her chest and groaning dramatically. Alice expected to open it to yet another message from David, groveling and pleading to have her back - either that or one that was littered with enough cussing to make Jonah Hill's eyes bleed.

She had been tempted to block David's number - even had her finger hovering over the button - but her curiosity had gotten the better of her. Alice wanted to see what other excuses, profanities, or stories he could dream up to text to her in his drunken stupors.

Whenever Alice thought of going back -
whenever she felt like picking up her phone and
calling him or asking him to come over - she just
looked back at his messages, and the irritation
drove her to reconsider. So far, it was working.
Alice's annoyance evaporated as soon as she
unlocked her phone. It was a reply from Mercer
Logistics, a major player in the tech business.
Alice had done a brief search before applying for
a position as a personal assistant. Quickly
learning that Mercer Logistics had their hands in
many different projects, nearly all of them
making use of a program, they developed
specifically to integrate with other service
providers.
She carefully reread the email. Twice.
They wanted her for an interview first thing
Monday. Alice squealed in happiness, hugging
her phone to her chest and grinning from ear to
ear. As soon as she caught her breath, another
bout of squealing and rolling around got her
flushed and winded.
She turned to her koala and buried her face in its

soft fur.

"Everything's gonna change for us, Beanie."

Chapter 2

Alice could see the hesitation in Alexa Mercer's face. She knew that look well. Every interview she had had that week was a colossal disappointment. Many of them never went further than the perfunctory greeting and the standard interview questions that included asking her where she saw herself in five years. Alice knew she didn't fit the profile of the people they usually hired. She was sure that Alexa Mercer was humoring her for the mandated fifteen minutes before pulling the plug as well. Alice inhaled deeply and put on her bravest face. She had done a dozen interviews in the last week, but this one had given her butterflies.

"I'm sorry, Miss Dean. An issue has come up, and I have to ask that we reschedule our interview," Alexa Mercer said.

No. Alice felt her stomach drop.

"Don't look so worried," Alexa said.

"I'm still more than happy to meet with you. The timing of this is just bad."

"What if I came with you?" Alice blurted.

"We can have a mobile interview, and when we're done, I'll just take an Uber home or something."

Alice was mortified, but the words had already left her lips, and she could not play them off or take them back. The look Alexa gave her made Alice wish she could crawl in a hole and die.

She must think I'm—

"Alright," Alexa beamed.

"Perfect," Alice replied.

***

Alice peeked at Alexa every so often as they weaved through traffic. The woman looked incredible in a dusty gray power suit. The color complimented her skin tone, and Alice found herself staring at the longest legs that she had ever seen.

"If you could be an animal, what would it

be?" Alexa suddenly asked.

"I'm sorry, what?" Alice questioned.

"I don't ask standard interview questions, Miss Dean. I want to know who I'm hiring, and I want to know if they will be an asset to my company."

"I see." Her nerves were strung tight, and her throat had gone dry.

Alexa turned off onto a dirt road. The trip hadn't taken nearly as long as she had hoped, and Alice fidgeted with the hem of her blouse.

"I..." Alice slammed down on her nervous energy and decided to answer honestly.

"A butterfly," Alice answered.

Alexa glanced at the girl sitting in the passenger seat as she brought the SUV to a stop and waited, the vehicle still running. Alexa took her in. Her dark hair was carefully and meticulously straightened. Her eyes darted around, looking at everything but directly at Alexa. While she didn't demand full attention, Alexa at least expected *some* eye contact, regardless of the stress factor. The girl's long-sleeved blouse was buttoned up nearly to her chin. Alexa glanced down at the cuffs and made out a small shape peeking out that could only be part of a tattoo. Alice was inexperienced in Alexa's industry. Alexa had carefully gone over the girl's application and resume before her interview, phoning the references listed to try and get a feel for her. While she seemed likable enough, and her references had given her a standard good-kid-who-works-hard review, Alexa couldn't quite get a read on her.

Alexa had to force herself to reserve judgment, but it was hard. It had been her cover letter that had gotten her to agree to the interview in the first place.

"A grubby little worm can grow up to be..." Alice struggled to find the word, frowning at her carefully painted nails.

"Majestic," Alice said. Alexa said nothing.

"They seem weak only compared to other, bigger creatures," Alice said, "but they move differently like they're in a separate world. And to see them, you have to slow down, and sometimes, they surprise you, because you had no idea they were there all along," Alice said, not satisfied with her rambly, followed Alexa's lead, and became quiet.

A man approached the vehicle, waving at Alexa, one hand holding his hardhat in place as he jogged over, tie flapping over his shoulder.

"Let's go," Alexa said, unbuckling. She disembarked smoothly, her suit completely wrinkle-free.

Alice, however, had some trouble and nearly fell out of the SUV. Her foot had caught on the booster step just outside the door.

Alice stood slightly back, listening as Alexa and the site manager discussed the issues that had arisen. He handed each of them a hardhat and jogged away.

"Do you know what it is we're doing here?" Alexa asked as she donned the hat.

"I'm not a hundred percent on the lingo," Alice admitted, recalling the conversation between Alexa and the site manager.

"But I am eager and willing to learn," she

hastily added when she saw Alexa's shoulders draw up ever so slightly, a tenseness around her mouth and eyes.

"It sounds like somewhere along the chain, communication was dropped, and the container never made it to site. Without the materials, the technological—um, the infrastructure that is required to make the integration between the parent company and Mercer Logistics possible isn't in place. The site can't go live until the container gets here, right?" Alice didn't stop for a breath.

"It's not just importing and distribution of physical materials," she added.

"I also know that you developed the systems that the parent company will be using." Alice indicated the logo on the corner of the giant board announcing the new home of the business.

"It's what put Mercer Logistics on the map." Alice paused, feeling lightheaded. She had wanted to blow Alexa away and not make her regret requesting the interview. Alice knew she was inexperienced in this industry, but she needed someone to give her a break. It usually just takes one person.

"The main draw is usually the systems. The rest are just nice little extras. The clients will order stock and materials once, maybe twice, if you're lucky, but get them to sign on to the system integration, and you've got a client for years. They'll turn to you for any other system queries and often stick with the company even if there is unprepared downtime. Why? Because not many other businesses in the industry can do what you can." Alice wiped her hands on her black jeans and turned to face Alexa.

"Look, I know I'm a little out of my league here, but I *am* the right fit. I've been working since I was sixteen, and I have held so many jobs, working my ass off to get anywhere, and if I stuck out working three, horrible, unsafe, inhumane—"
She cut herself off, closed her eyes, and slowly, very carefully formed her last few sentences.

"I know that you built the company from the ground up, and even though you could probably have sold Mercer Logistics to the highest bidder and retired early, you stayed because you know what makes this place tick."

Alexa tilted her head and suppressed a smile.

Alice was smart, and she had shown a knack for stripping away the fluff to expose the baseline of information.

Alice paused again, gathered herself, and added, "I'm worth your time."

"Good girl," Alexa said, a smile finally breaking across her face. Alice stopped talking, her face flushed. The change was subtle, but it was noticeable. Alice had gone from this punk, almost-forceful, self-assured woman to a soft little girl.

Alice bit her lower lip, lowering her gaze to the floor, suppressing a smile. Her face was still burning. She shook her head slightly and lifted her gaze to Alexa's.

The wind caught Alice's hair and fanned it out, affording Alexa a flash of pink.

Alice's body tingled at the way Alexa looked at her. It was a combination of surprise and desire.

It caused a hot flush to pulse through her.

"We're done here," Alexa said, signing off on something and handed it over to the site manager who had appeared out of nowhere. She turned to Alice, taking in the demure, fragile expression on her face.

"I still have some questions for you, so if you've got the time, I'd like to continue our interview in a slightly more relaxed setting." Her face lit up, and Alexa found herself pleased at the girl's response.

"Absolutely!"

***

After Alice left, Alexa's mind brought up that very innocent look on Alice's—her pink cheeks and the pleased smile on her face.
Her subtle submission had sent a thrill through Alexa. The girl's knowledge had surprised her. Alexa shifted in her chair as she stared absentmindedly out of her office window. Alice had visibly relaxed when they were in a familiar

place. She had recommended a small coffee shop where the staff greeted her like she was a part of their family.

Full of surprises, Alice had offered to pay for their drinks and insisted on paying their server's tip even after the owner comped their coffee and pie.

She looked down at her desk, where Alexa had the potential candidates lined up next to one another. Alexa had been making notes on each of them before her mind had wandered. Alexa tapped the pen on the application she was on. It was Alice's. Along the margins were notes and memos to herself about how her interview had gone.

Alexa had already discarded many applications, and at first glance, Alice would have followed the same fate, but she had stood out more than the rest. She seemed to be a genuine and kind person. Alexa had noticed a slight shift in demeanor when her family and home life was brought up, but Alice had glossed over it and had tactfully diverted the topic.

Although her work experience came across as a tad excessive, Alexa appreciated that no matter where she had worked, she had stayed as long as it proved beneficial. She was torn between taking a chance on this little girl and going with someone certain to know what they were doing. Yawning, Alexa switched her computer screen off and rolled her chair back in one smooth movement. It was already dark outside, long after everyone had already gone home for the day. She glanced back at the short stack of potential candidates. Her mind told her to choose the more mature, straight-laced lady that had experience in managing an office and running different departments.

On the other hand, there was Alice.

Alice was young and smart and had blown Alexa away at the site today. Usually, Alexa would sit on the decision for a few days to make sure she wasn't jumping the gun. She analyzed every aspect of every decision, but today her gut was telling her to throw her analytical side out the window and go with the girl.

John, Alexa's husband, continuously teased her about Alexa's inability to make snap decisions. He would almost always make huge, dramatic displays of exasperation when they were out together. She knew he was just teasing her goodnaturedly, and she loved that he was able to keep her grounded.

Alexa glanced at her watch, tapped her freshly manicured nail on the glass, and reached for the phone.

***

"May I please speak with Miss Dean?" Alice sat up, nervous energy sparking inside of her.

"This is she."

"Miss Dean, this is Alexa Mercer."

"Oh," Alice's heart dropped a little, "How can I help?" She fiddled with Beanie in her lap, already bracing herself for the inevitable.

"I'd like you to come in tomorrow to go over some paperwork."

"Paperwork?" Alice questioned.

A soft, light laugh on the other line made her stomach clench unhappily.

"Does that mean..." Alice trailed off, hoping that Alexa would fill in the rest.

"Yes, Miss Dean. You've got the job."

Alice flopped back onto her bed after hanging up the phone, her ears still ringing. Did that happen?

"I thought I blew it," Alice said to herself, her mind reeling. She covered her face with a pillow and let out a squeal, kicking her legs. Alice hugged the pillow to her chest. She stared up at the ceiling, catching her breath and grinning from ear to ear.

Her mind then replayed the moment Alexa Mercer had called her a good girl. Then she thought about it again and again. She recalled the way her body had tingled and how easily she nearly slipped into her little space. There was this energy that Alexa Mercer gave off that simultaneously set her at ease and made her nervous. She was eager to please her. She wanted

Alexa to call her a good girl again, and Alice found herself imagining Alexa praising her as she satisfied her.

Chapter 3

Alice arrived to work before everyone else. She sat at her desk chair and waited, feeling out of her depth. Swiveling in her seat, she found the quiet to be slightly eerie. Alice hopped off to make some coffee and felt her pull-up shift uncomfortably beneath her skirt. Alice tried to wiggle it back into submission, but her it was sitting too tightly to move that way. She prepared the coffee machine and grimaced again as her pull-up pinched her skin. Alice hastily made her way to the bathroom, not wanting to take up too much time. She lifted her skirt and pinned the end of it under her chin as she shuffled the pull-up free and fixed her slip. She heard the coffee machine whistle a tune, and she hastily dropped her skirt, rushing from the bathroom.

Alexa half-glanced up from the document she had been poring over and paused as Alice appeared in front of her. Alexa turned her full attention to the girl.

She looked stunning in a frilled emerald green button-up blouse and a black skirt. Alexa let her eyes wander, and a smile spread to her lips. Alice's skirt was tucked into her pull-up. A rush of excitement flashed through her as she absently dropped the contract she was reading over onto the desk beside her and stepped closer to Alice.

"Here," she said. Alice looked up at Alexa, startled by how close she was standing.

"Wh—" Alice's face flushed a deep, hot red. Alexa had reached down and was gently tugging her skirt out of her pull-up. Alice felt embarrassment rise like a tidal wave inside of her. Alexa brushed her hand over Alice's rear, feeling the thicker material of the pull up beneath as she smoothed out the material of her skirt.

"There you go," Alexa said, giving Alice a knowing half-smile. She placed the softest of touches on Alice's cheek, "We don't want people to see your little secret."

Alice let out a surprised squeak and flushed a brighter scarlet.

"I won't tell if you don't," Alexa said, raising an eyebrow to the speechless Alice.

***

Alexa was positively thrilled at how subdued Alice was after their run-in outside of the bathroom. The subtle changes in her behavior belied her submissive nature. Alexa grinned as she remembered the pull-up. Little Alice certainly had surprised her.

Alice hadn't interacted with Alexa much after that, avoiding her gaze and furiously blushing when she caught Alexa staring. Alice busied herself with anything within reach to avoid catching Alexa's eye. Her body was still tingling from her touch. What had caught Alice by complete surprise wasn't that Alexa had seemed okay with seeing one of her employees in a pull-up, but rather that Alice had *liked* that it was her boss that had seen her.

"Alice," Alexa said, standing much too close to her, forcing the girl to look up at her through her.

Gosh, her eyes are gorgeous, Alexa thought to herself.

"Yes, Mrs. Mercer?"

"Call me Alexa," she said, her voice betraying her attraction. Alice swallowed.

"Yes, Alexa."

"Good girl," Alexa said, watching her face flush a second time.

"Did Thomas from accounting send the breakdown yet?"

"No, M— Alexa," Alice said, correcting herself. The approval on Alexa's face did something funny to her, as did her close presence. Alice could feel her arousal pool between her legs each time Alexa looked at her.

"Get him up here for me, won't you?"

"Yes, Alexa."

"Perfect, and when you're done with that, come see me in my office," Alexa said. Alice's heart stalled.

"Deep breath, Alice. You're not in trouble." Alexa saw the immediate relief on her face and suppressed a smile.

Alice is such a baby, Alexa thought.

"I want to show you how to begin managing my day-to-day as soon as possible," Alex explained. Alice nodded, "Is there anything else you need?" Alice softly asked. Alexa thought for a moment.

"Not right now, you've been such a good girl," Alexa cooed. Alice, feeling a head-spinning arousal build inside of her.

Chapter 4

"John," Alexa said. The tone of her voice drew his attention immediately. He looked up from his guitar, the pick still between his teeth, to look at her. His brow was furrowed in concern. He carefully set his instrument down and removed the pick.

"John. You wouldn't believe how adorable the new girl is," Alexa gushed.

"Annie?"

"Alice," Alexa corrected.

"She blew me away in the interview, and today, oh my gosh."
John smiled, curious, leaning forward in his seat, "What on Earth happened?"

"She wore a pull-up."

"What?" John's voice was louder than he had intended.

"Yes!"

"There was just this *vibe*, you know?" Alexa said.

"She had a wardrobe malfunction, and I

reached down and helped her."

John watched as his wife's face glowed. She started describing how distracting it had been after she had fixed little Alice's pull-up.

"She was so different after that - so demure - and her blushing cheeks were too cute not to touch," Alexa sighed deeply and grinned.

"I think you'd love her, John."

"Really?"

"I think she has an Instagram account," Alexa said, excited to share her find with her husband. She bounced up off the couch to fetch her tablet from the home office. John shook his head and smiled.

"She must be something special for you to go on about her like this."

Alexa returned with her tablet in hand, her eyes glittering with wild excitement, "She's perfect; smart and cute, and..." Alexa paused as she clicked on Alice's profile.

"See."

The girl was stunning. Her chocolate brown hair hung straight past her shoulders, her equally alluring eyes staring right through him. Her lips were small but full, and her smile promised him wonder-filled days.

"Wow," he breathed.

They scrolled through her posts, landing on one where she was dressed in a white onesie, posing cutely for the camera. Her breasts were perfect for her slight build. He admired the tropical tattoos on her thigh. Alice's pose reminded him of a little girl caught doing naughty things, and it stirred heat through him. John lifted Alexa easily, setting her on his lap, her back to his chest, "Did she turn you on?" John felt her squirm, a slow smile spreading across his face.

"Tell me what you want to do to her, Alexa," John murmured in her ear. Her body was pressed against him, and he could feel himself grow hard. He ran his hands over her front, unbuttoning her blouse.

Alexa inhaled sharply, her body tingling. She bit her lip as she eyed the picture on her screen, glancing over her shoulder at him. She recognized the light in his eyes, and it sent a shiver through her.

He unclasped the front catch of her bra and lightly bit her ear, growling. His wife's breathing changed, and he felt her nipples grow hard beneath his touch.

"Tell me," he demanded.

"I want her to call me, Mommy," Alexa moaned. John slowly slid his hand down her smooth belly, dipping his hand below the waistband of her skirt.

"Do you want her to touch you?" John asked, stroking the soft skin above the elastic of her underwear.

"Yes," she said breathlessly.

"I want you to touch her," John whispered.

"While you watch?" Alexa's face turned a delicious shade of pink as she thought it over. Her mind wandered to the look on Alice's face when Alexa had sensually pressed herself against the girl while pulling her pull-up into place.

"What if she offered to please her, Daddy? Would you just watch then?" Alexa groaned and gyrated against him.

"Do you want her to suck on your nipples?" John asked, pinching her nipple, eliciting a moan from her.

"Just imagine bathing her, running a washcloth over that pale, soft skin of hers," John whispered, running his tongue over Alexa's earlobe. Alexa's skirt rode up as she straddled him, grinding against his swelling cock, exposing the warm, caramel skin of her thighs. John's eyes landed on the lace of her underwear, and he felt his cock jerk.
He pulled his hand free and stroked her thighs.

"Imagine little Alice standing for you to rub lotion onto her skin after a bath."
Alexa leaned back into him, running the palm of her hand over his bulge, her cheeks flushed, and her nipples hard.

"I want you, John." His erection pressed uncomfortably against the zipper of his jeans. He gripped her by the waist, pressing himself against her core, delighting in the soft moan that escaped.

"Right here?" John asked, his voice hoarse. Alexa nodded, her mind swirling. He slid the back of his hand over her mound, moisture already making her panties stick to her swollen lips. He pressed a fingertip against her, massaging her clit. Alexa bit back a moan, leaning her head back.

"Imagine little Alice touching you like this," John said. Alexa moaned again, and he grinned. John slipped his fingertips beneath the elastic of her panties, and his wife shuddered. He teased her, stroking the skin around the edges of her underwear, chills erupting over her skin.

"Imagine little Alice on her knees in front of you, her tongue trailing up your thigh to your pussy."

"Why are you teasing me?" Alexa moaned, the rough, calloused fingers sending shivers through her, her body burning for more of his touch.

"I want you to beg," John said, pulling her closer with his free hand, planting kisses along the nape of her neck. Goosebumps exploded over her skin, and Alexa moaned loudly, grinding against his hand.

"I want you to imagine teaching little Alice how to please me."

He held her waist, keeping her still as Alexa growled at him, "Stop teasing me."

Alexa saw the glint in his eyes and the smirk that spread across his face at her words. Alexa fought against his hold, needing his touch to soothe her.

"No, no," John said grinning.

Frustrated, Alexa pressed herself against him, hovering her lips over his. She felt him stiffen as his fingers dug into her soft flesh.

"I can tease, too," Alexa whispered, her lips still barely touching his.

John's cock pulsed, and his breathing became heavy. Alexa knew exactly what drove him insane, and he loved it.

"Careful, Alexa."

Alexa leaned back so he could see her face. She pulled her bottom lip between her teeth and tilted her head in a cutesy way, challenging him to resist. She leaned forward again and flicked her tongue over his bottom lip.

It got the response she had wanted. John groaned and pressed his groin against hers, his hands holding her tightly against him as he thrust against her. His response sent a wave of pleasure coursing through her veins. His urgency ignited her, and a flashfire of hot need tore through her. Alexa grinned, her eyes flashing at him.

John stood, his strong arms bulging as he lifted Alexa effortlessly. With one hand, he held her to him, and with the other, he unbuttoned and unzipped his jeans, freeing his rock-hard cock. He shoved her panties aside and lowered her down, her moist, warm pussy gripping him tightly as he pushed into her.

Alexa inhaled as she took his full length into her, feeling his hardness fill her up. All thoughts of teasing him had dissolved in desire. Alexa pressed her lips against his and suckled on his lower lip, begging for more.

John groaned at the taste of her, his cock hard and throbbing, pleasure guiding his slow thrusts

as he pushed himself deeper into his wife.
Alexa's moans spurred him on, and he felt a
familiar tightening of his balls. He pulled out,
wanting to make their encounter last as long as
possible.

"No," Alexa whimpered as he pulled away.

"Relax, my love. We're not done yet."

"What are you doing?" He set her down
on the couch, pushing her skirt up to her belly
and pulling her panties down.

Alexa gasped as the cold leather of the couch,
touched the bare skin of her ass. John stuffed her
underwear into the pocket of his jeans and
spread her legs wide.

"I want you to scream my name," John
said as he lowered his face to her pussy, his
tongue flicking over her clit.

"I want you to imagine little Alice doing
this to you."

Alexa's body twitched, and a whimper escaped
her lips.

"Imagine her pleasing her, Mommy.
Imagine her being pleased just like this."

Her body was flushed, tingling. Her mind a whirl of thoughts of John and Alice.

"John," Alexa breathed, her eyes unable to focus. She grasped the backrest of the couch for support.

"Tell me what you want, Alexa," John said, his fingers slowly circling her dripping core, his thumb massaging her clit. He pushed a finger inside of her, drawing a soft moan from her lips. He inserted one more and drew yet another moan from her lips. Alexa arched her back.

"John, I want you."

He brought his lips to her moist folds and suckled on her, flicking his tongue over her clit. Her scent was making cum drip from the head of his cock, but he held back. He wanted Alexa to ask for it.

"I need your cock," Alexa said, her moan turning into a heavy whimper.

"Where do you need it?"

"I want your throbbing cock inside of my pussy, John. I want you to fuck me."

John's cock jerked violently, and he had to

clench his jaw to keep from cumming. He continued to massage his wife's clit as he pressed the head of his cock against her opening. Alexa let out a low growl of anticipation.

He pushed his cock into her moist heat, and Alexa's body clenched around him, pulsing lightly as she edged her orgasm.

"Oh, yes," Alexa moaned.

"Don't you dare cum yet, Alexa." He draped himself over her, drinking in her scent, planting kisses against her neck and cheek as she met his slow thrusts, quivering beneath him.

"I love you," Alexa whispered into his ear as she gently scraped her nails down his back. She felt John's cock throb once, and he had to slow his thrusts to keep himself controlled.

"I love you," he said, rubbing his face in her neck.

He gently bit down on her shoulder, and she panted.

Their bodies were warm, glittering with a fine sheen of sweat and sex as they rocked together. His cock swelled, and he growled in her ear,

"Cum for me. I want to feel it on my cock." Alexa bit down on a loud moan as her body exploded around his cock. Her pussy clenched tightly, pulsing around him, milking him as he continued to draw her orgasm out.
John pulled out, slowly, watching as bliss and pleasure played across her face.

"How was that, Mommy?" John winked at her.

"I've got so much more planned, Alexa," John whispered, massaging her breasts, running his thumbs over her nipples.
John and Alexa laid on the bed in the dark, panting, and still entwined. Alexa pressed her face into his neck and inhaled his scent and heat. Her body was still twitching and thrumming.

"Fuck." Alexa laughed.

"Want to do that again?" Alexa asked. She raised her eyebrows at him, her hand already scraping along the dusting of dark, prickly hair running from his navel to the base of his cock before stroking him again.

Alice dropped her bag on the kitchen counter and kicked her shoes off. Her body was wired. She had been begging to be touched all day. After the incident with Alexa, Alice had found it hard to concentrate on her work, stealing glances at Alexa whenever she stopped by. She recalled the way Alexa's hands felt on her skin as she helped fix her skirt. She remembered the hungry look in her eyes when she called her 'little Alice.' Alice's heart thumped wildly. She grabbed her laptop and set it on the edge of her bed, waiting for it to boot up as she stripped off her work clothes and walked around her apartment naked. Her work clothes were so restrictive.

She opened the link and stared. Her personal Instagram had nearly a thousand posts. Alice scrolled through them, admiring the beauty of each shot. Alice leaned forward and looked at the photo of Alexa with her husband, reading that his name was John. She paused at one where John was looking straight at the camera, guitar in hand. His dusty blonde hair was hanging over one side of his face, and there was a guitar pick between his teeth. A tremor went through her body. He was hot, and Alice licked her lips her, recognizing him. She had been to most of his local performances, delighting in the way the music had made her feel and losing herself in the lyrics. Alice spent some time going through his photos, each one highlighting his form. She felt moisture pool between her legs while at the same time, a hot vibration shuddered through her core. There was one where he and his wife were lying in bed, hair mussed, sheets hinting at their naked forms beneath. Alice's hand slipped between her legs, absently running her fingers over her swollen mound, moistening her panties. Alice opened Alexa's account, and her heart hammered in her chest. The woman had a body to die for. Her account showed posts of her everyday life, from having coffee in bed with John to sitting poolside in the smallest bikini known to man, showing off every dip and curve. The next one had Alexa dressed in nothing but a slightly-too-big leather jacket and aviator sunglasses. Alice moaned out loud when she read a caption on the photo: *Mommy knows you've been bad, baby.*

Chapter 5

"Rats," Alice muttered, shaking the contents of her purse out onto her desk.

"What?" Alexa asked, her eyes skimming over a document as she walked up behind her.

"Oh, it's nothing," Alice said, hastily trying to shove her things back into the empty bag. Alexa eyed the mess and arched her brow.

"I forgot my wallet," Alice relented, and she laughed at her little slip-up.

"I guess that's what I get for going to bed at three in the morning."

"What were you doing up so late?" Alexa asked. Alice managed to hide the fact that her cheeks had turned pink by faking a coughing fit.

"Just Netflix," Alice mumbled. She took a drink of water.

"Lunch is on me," Alexa said.

"What, no. I can't."

"Can't eat?" Alexa asked grinning. She pulled a couple of fifties from her pocket and stuffed them into Alice's hands before she could protest further.

"Thanks," Alice said, taken back by Alexa's generosity.

"A good little girl would get a spanking for leaving something so important at home," Alexa murmured and held on to her. Alice's eyes grew wide, and she took the smallest of steps back, her heart beginning to race.

"You want Mommy to spank you, Alice?" Alexa asked, pressing herself closer to her. Alexa could feel herself getting aroused. The blush on Alice's face certainly didn't help the situation.

"I can promise you that punishment would be in order if you were my little girl," Alexa murmured. Alice moaned, quivering at the thought, her knees weakening. Alice didn't know if Alexa had put her arms around her, and that was why her knees gave out or if Alexa had caught her. There was an unmistakable glint of lust in Alexa's gaze as she breathed into her ear.

"Just imagine me pulling you over my lap and spanking you for being a naughty girl." Alice licked her lips as she stared into Alexa's eyes.

Alexa leaned in ever so slightly.

"Alexa, call for you on line three," a boxy, scratchy voice announced, breaking the tension. Annoyed, Alexa reached past Alice and pressed the button on the intercom. Without breaking eye contact with Alice, she asked, "Who is it?"

"Geoff from DigiTech," the voice replied.

"Fine, I'll shift some meetings. Put him through to my office," Alexa said.

"Yes, Alexa."

"Get yourself a little treat too, Alice." Alice stared at Alexa's lips, feeling her belly do a little flip when she said her name.

***

Alice's eyes kept drifting over to Alexa. She was on the phone with a supplier. Her hair pulled into a neat bun instead of the loose locks they had been this morning. Alice dropped her gaze to Alexa's breasts, and thoughts of her suckling on them came unbidden to her. Alice chewed on her lip as she imagined her tongue flicking over her boss' nipples, sucking them. She shifted in her seat, pressing her thighs together, trying to lessen the pressure between her legs. Her mind drifted to John and Alexa together, and her face flushed a bright scarlet. Alexa caught her gaze and smirked. Alice hastily looked away from her, her heart pounding. She kept replaying Alexa's words in her mind, loving the way Alexa had called herself Mommy. Alice allowed herself to think about what it would be like to have Alexa as her Mommy and to have Alexa help her change into her onesie after a nice warm bath.

"Distracted?" Alexa asked from right behind her. Alice jumped a little in her seat, "No. Of course not." Alexa saw color streak across her cheeks, turning her ears bright red. She grinned, "Of course not." Alexa pressed her legs against Alice's, delighting in the warmth of her skin, "You wouldn't want to get into trouble again, would you?" She looked up at Alexa, her height and heels forcing her to tilt her head back. Alice shook her head ever so slightly, her big submissive eyes making Alexa's heart pound.

"Good," Alexa said, stepping away from her, continuing on her way to yet another meeting as if nothing had just transpired between them.

***

Alice leaned against her apartment door, keys still in hand.

"Oh, gosh." Alice giggled, then burst out laughing.

"I'm so screwed." Alice slid down to the floor, still laughing, her heart thumping wildly inside her chest. When her hysterics died down, Alice got to her feet.

"I am *so* screwed." Her mind wandered again to an image of Alexa as she leaned on her desk, sensually rubbing her thighs together as she talked to her husband over the phone. She could swear that Alexa's touch lingered on Alice's skin.

Her body tingled, reminding her of the way Alexa had made her feel, reminding her of the fact that

she'd been soaking through her panties all day.
Alice absentmindedly unbuttoned her blouse, the
cool air causing her nipples to harden beneath
her bra. Her mind recalled the incident with
Alexa at lunch.

Good girl. Alice imagined Alexa was right
there with her.

*Mommy knows you've been bad, baby
girl.*

She rubbed her clit, her eyes locked on Alexa's as
she imagined her pulling her over her lap,
spanking her for staying up past her bedtime.
Her legs were shaking. Alice closed her eyes and
imagined the feel of Alexa's breasts against her
bare skin. She slipped her fingers past her
panties and slowly pushed them inside her.

*Are you going to be a naughty little girl
again? You know naughty little girls get
punished.*

Alice's breathing sped up, her orgasm drawing
closer as Alexa's words echoed in her head.
Alice's body tightened around her fingers, and
sparks exploded behind her lids as she came,

hard. She stayed where she was, her fingers still inside her core, letting that floaty feeling wash over her.

"Yep. Definitely screwed."

Chapter 6

"Miss Dean? Are you still there?" Came the man's voice down the phone. Alice felt the blood rush to her head while it pounded painfully in her ears and behind her eyes. Her throat tightened, and her heart was racing.

"Yes," Alice choked out.

"Do you have someone who can drive you?" The voice asked.

"Um," Alice blinked slowly and stupidly. Her heart was torn in two directions, and it made her stomach swirl nauseatingly.

"What's the address? I'll be there soon," Alice replied.

***

The unpleasantness of everything was overwhelming. Alice felt dizzy as she waited outside the morgue. She buried everything—the fresh wave of emotion that came when she'd gotten the call, everything. It was too much. She

had numbed herself to all that was around her,
building a wall, feeling muted and blocked off.
And when she stood over them, she felt nothing.
Alice knew that she would feel guilty about it
later, but at that moment, there was nothing.

"It's them," Alice confirmed with the
coroner.

"Where—" She caught herself, "No, I'd
rather not know." The man nodded and filled out
the paperwork. Alice left the room, clutching her
keys so tightly that they cut painfully into her
hand.

***

Alice kept wiping her hands on her jeans, her
fingertips cold, and her head hurting from
tension. She wiped her hands another time and
compared the address to the one she had saved
on her phone.

She remained in her car, just staring at the faded
blue door that set their house apart from the
matchboxes beside it. Alice forced herself to turn

off the car and get out. Otherwise, she would be there all night.

At first, she just stood on the sidewalk staring at the small, unassuming house that lay between similarly modest and dingy-looking houses. Then she took small, shaky steps toward it. The distance between the sidewalk and the front door stretched out further with each step, feeling like hours had passed, until, suddenly, reality snapped back into place, and she found herself standing right in front of the door much sooner than she had wished. Alice hesitated on the threshold. The house seemed to grow taller and scarier, looming over her. She had been on her own since she was sixteen. She hadn't expected the place to be still standing ten years after the fact. Alice hadn't been back since the night her mom had screeched at her to get out. A cold sweat broke out on her back as she unlocked the door to the small rental house. She slowly pushed it open. It was like walking through a door to the past. Memories assaulted her, and she wiped her palms on her jeans over and over again, no longer feeling anything but the burn in her stomach.

I wish I got rid of you like my Mom had wanted me to!

Her mom's voice repeated in her mind, the pain echoing dully. Her dad had been too high to care. To be fair, it was a normal state for both of them, but that night, Lena had thrown ashtrays and other objects at her. Glass and ceramics had shattered around her. Alice blinked. Nothing had changed except, perhaps, the fact that less personal things and more trash were lying around than she remembered. The divot in the wall was still there where the second ashtray had sailed over her head the night she had left.

"You can do this," Alice said to herself as she fought with a stack of flattened boxes. The silence in the house caused an unpleasant chill to travel through her.

It smelled stale. Another memory assailed her. She recalled coming home from school with a friend and finding her mom so coked up that she just stared blankly at them, gently rocking herself where she sat on the kitchen floor, drooling on herself. It was also the last time she had invited a friend over.

***

The last room was hers. When Alice had left home, she had taken only a small handful of things. Alice was surprised to see that they had left her space virtually untouched. Virtually, because anything of value had been stripped and sold off, no doubt for money to fund their habits or to pay rent, but the rest had been left in, more or less, the same place.

She couldn't breathe due to pressure in her chest. Alice forced one foot in front of the other as she entered deeper into the room. There was a distinct smell of old, stale air and smoke that had filtered and soaked into everything. Alice dragged an empty box into the room behind her and stood idly in the center, her mind a whirl of emotions and flashes of memories. She felt a strange, familiar echoing emptiness, and she found herself looking down at her body in that room, automatically beginning the process of clearing it out. She folded the ratty bedding and shook the dust from a pillow. She then stuffed them into a trash bag. She would donate these, she thought. Other small knick-knacks that were worthless to her parents had gathered a layer of dust and discolored the wood and plastic. There was a little wooden bird her dad had carved for her when she was three. The wood was dry and cracked. She picked it up carefully. The wood was rough beneath her fingertips, and she had a memory of her dad pointing out bright red plumage of the robin he was copying. She had giggled happily, squealing and shaking her already-thin arms. A vicious reminder invaded her mind. There may have been sweet moments interspersed with the bad, but this had never been her home. They hadn't wanted her. Alice grew angry, and her hand tightened around the small figurine.

"Just throw it away," she said to the empty room.

"I should just throw it all away."
Alice leaned her head against her knees and whispered to herself, "Why am I even here?" She looked again at the small bird and squashed the impulse to destroy it. She carefully placed it at the top of the box with a handful of other odds and ends, and then she taped it shut. Her clothes wouldn't fit her anymore, so she opted to donate those, too. Alice cleaned up her room much faster than she had anticipated. There hadn't been much of her left in that place, anyway. Alice struggled and tilted the bed onto its side, upsetting a couple of daddy long leg spiders as they wobbled away, hastily over the dusty carpet. She gathered the scraps of paper, stray socks, and clumps of dust bunnies. She gave the room a good once-over, making sure that everything had been packed up. The curtains were faded and just as dusty as everything else in the room. She would take those down after running a vacuum through the place. She vaguely considered getting a service to come out and clean the hole for her, but Alice knew that even had she been

paid, she couldn't afford to spend frivolously. Alice had separated everything that she was going to donate from the things she could sell or would keep. The rest of the boxes were stacked neatly up against the wall by the front door. There hadn't been very much to clear out, but it still amounted to a couple of boxes of keepsakes, junk, and various items, books, and stacks of yellowed photos she couldn't bear to sort through yet. She did call a service to collect the things she was going to donate. They collected for free, and since they hailed from the area, the trip wouldn't cost them very much in terms of fuel. Alice helped the older man load the things into his truck.

"Thank you for collecting these things, sir," she said numbly.

"Thank you for donating them to us, missy. As you know, we are more than happy to take them." Alice took her last $50 from her pocket and handed it to him after everything was loaded. She had given them the mattresses as well, sure that someone else could make better use of them than she could.

"You've given so much, miss," the old man said, his eyes wide. No doubt, he had taken in the general look of the neighborhood and had drawn his conclusions regarding her financial situation. While it was true that she wasn't living quite as comfortably as she wanted, she wasn't living the way she had growing up in this house. Alice no longer went to bed hungry.

"Please, it's not much, but I want you to have it."

His old eyes softened, and he wrapped his warm wrinkled hands around hers, thanking her again, taking the offering.

She didn't wait for him to leave before returning to the house. She loaded the boxes in her car and went back inside, standing in the empty living room/kitchen. The sun was already setting, a chill creeping into the house. Alice had briefly considered sleeping in there, but she had already broken her promise of never returning. She wasn't about to fall asleep in a house she hated, surrounded by memories that would choke her to death while she slept.

After some deliberation, Alice spent the night sleeping upright in her car.

She spent the greater majority of the weekend packing, cleaning, and dealing with the legal paperwork and meetings that were required in situations such as hers. She had them cremated but didn't bother picking them up from the funeral home. She drove home in the dark, not once glancing back at the darkened windows of her parents' crappy house.

***

"Morning, Alice," Alexa said, smiling brightly. Alice smiled, the action feeling hollow and rehearsed, "Morning, Alexa." If Alexa had noticed the lack of warmth in her tone, she didn't acknowledge it. Alice watched her walk into her office and close the door behind her.

Good, Alice thought. She wouldn't be able to force a smile or convince anyone she was okay for too long. Remaining numb was what was keeping her upright at the moment, and the less she thought and felt, the better.

Before lunch, Alexa buzzed her, "Alice, could you please bring me DigiTech's file?"

"Here, Alexa." Alice said as she entered after a quick, soft knock.

"Is there anything else?" Alice asked. Alexa looked at her, and Alice felt her gaze bore through her much like she had that first day they met.

"Is there something on your mind?" Alexa asked tentatively.

"If you're not happy with the work, we can figure something out."
Alice shook her head, "The work is great, Alexa, really..." She stopped herself, feeling the familiar tightness in her throat. She forced a smile, "I'm just a little tired. I didn't sleep well." It wasn't entirely a lie. Alexa didn't press. Alice was entitled to her privacy.

"I'll have Gabe order us something from the Greek deli down the street. They have the best coffee." Alexa offered. Alice nodded, the fake smile still on her lips, "That sounds great. Thank you, Alexa."

***

Alexa watched her carefully as she stirred sugar into her coffee. It was too much for her taste, but she knew that Alice had a liking for sweet things. Her instinct was to hold Alice's smaller frame in her arms and rock her until she fell asleep. She felt a tug inside her heart and kept trying to connect to Alice, but Alice wasn't letting her in. Alexa didn't want to let her go home tonight if she wasn't sure of her mental state.

"How was your weekend, Alice? Didn't you say you were going to go out with some friends?" Alexa probed, watching her face closely. The smile dropped away, and the cup lowered from her face.

"I..." Alice's voice grew thick, and she cleared her throat. "I was..."

"Alice?" Alexa asked, leaning forward,

"Are you okay?" Alice felt the wave of tears rise and break over her. They welled up inside her, obscuring her vision, and choking her.

"I'm..." *Fine.* The word died in her throat, and she swallowed against the tightness in her chest. She felt as if she was going to vibrate apart.

"Would it be okay if I hugged you?" Alexa asked. Alice's body was shaking, but in a fragile state of mind, even the kindest touch could cause mental and physical distress if the person did not want to be touched. Alice nodded. The moment Alexa's arms wrapped around her, she lost her composure. She buried her head against Alexa's shoulder and cried. Everything she had held in over the last ten years, ever since she left that house, came out in one great flood. She sobbed, shaking, and unable to breathe through the tears and the screams.

"Shh, it's okay," Alexa said, stroking her hair. She could feel Alice's tears soak into her shirt, but Alexa didn't care. When Alice's sobs finally quieted, she looked at Alexa apologetically.

"Here," Alexa said, handing her a makeup wipe and several tissues.

"I'm sorry. I didn't mean to just fall apart like that."

"Don't be, Alice," Alexa said and patted her arm, "We need to let our emotions out, or they'll hide in our hearts until we shatter." Alice cleaned herself up, using Alexa's compact mirror to make sure the streaks of mascara and eyeliner were cleanly wiped away.

"So, tell me what happened, Alice. Please. I want to help," Alexa almost begged. Alice nodded, drying her eyes.

"My parents died over the weekend." Alice didn't know how to finish her thought, "I hadn't been back there since I was sixteen."

"I take it you didn't have the best relationship with them?" Alexa questioned. Alice shook her head.

"Do you have other family?" Alexa looked at Alice with compassion.

"My aunt, but she wasn't on speaking

terms with my mom. I was the only one they could reach." She dropped her head in her hands and sighed, pulling her fingers through her hair as she looked at Alexa.

"Come on," Alexa said, holding her hand out to Alice.

"I think we should get out of here. Get you home."

Alice shook her head, her eyes finding the pattern on the carpet beneath her feet.

"You can't stay here all night, Alice," Alexa said, her voice firm but kind.

Alice looked up at her, surprised at how easily she allowed Alexa to take control.

Alexa called one of the clerks into her office.

"Please arrange that Miss Dean's vehicle is delivered to her residence. I'm taking her home."

"Yes, Mrs. Mercer."

Alexa held her hand out to Alice again, a soft smile on her face.

"Please?" Alice hesitantly took it.

"Thank you, Alexa," Alice whispered.

***

"Buckle your seatbelt, please," Alexa said. Alice's hands were shaking too much, "I..." She stopped, feeling her instinctual response to keep her little side hidden. The stress was too much, and she could feel her brain clench tightly in response. Alice didn't want to go home. Alice looked at Alexa with new tears in her eyes, pleading silently.

"Here," Alexa said, leaning over and clipping the buckle in place. Alexa's flowery scent filled her nose, and she whispered a small thank you.

"Where do you live?" Alexa asked. Alice shook her head.

"I don't want to go home. I can't." She remembered the unpacked boxes waiting for her when she did eventually get there. She shook her head again, more firmly than before.

"Then I'm taking you home with me," Alexa said, settling the matter.

"I don't think you should be alone,

anyway." Alice nodded. They spent the ride home in silence, Alice feeling her mind pull back from her emotions again, too tired to talk or think.

***

"Drink your tea, sweetie," Alexa said kindly, "It'll warm you up." Alice automatically did as she was told; her eyes still red from tears. She had felt embarrassed at first, having broken down in front of her boss, but Alexa didn't seem to mind it at all. Alexa was kind and caring and had let her be.

"Good girl," Alexa said with a smile. Alice felt her heart thump once, and new tears threatened to fall.

"Do you want to talk about it?" John asked, his gray eyes warm. He touched her cheek, wiping away a stray tear. It was a nice type of weird to be meeting John amidst her most vulnerable place. Alice shook her head. Then, after a few moments, she nodded.

"I don't know." Her voice cracked, becoming softer.

"It's okay," John said. He looked at his wife.

"Alexa and I—we're here for you. Whatever you need. We'll take care of you, okay?" Alice wished in her heart that it was true, and when she met their gazes, she believed them. There was not a single trace of judgment or disgust coming from them.

"Promise?" Alice asked, her voice light and small, tears spilling over again.

"Promise," John said. Alice threw her arms around him and sobbed for the second time in less than an hour. Alexa smiled, her heart warmed by the sight of John's tenderness as he stroked Alice's hair and let her tears soak through his favorite shirt.

"I'll run you a nice warm bath, Alice. Would you like that?" John asked her. Alice nodded, still sobbing.

"Come with me," Alexa said, leading Alice to the master bedroom and en-suite bathroom.

Alice was barely able to take in the design and beauty of the place. Her head was fuzzy, and her eyes burned. Alexa's hand was wrapped around hers, and she stared down at it. She was shaking, scared, and sad. Alice wished she didn't have these feelings for her parents. She hated them, and she loved them, and she wished that her life had been different from the start. When Alice just stood numbly in front of the bubble-filled tub, Alexa touched her hand again, drawing her attention.

"Can you stay with me?" Alice asked.

"Of course, Alie."

Alice's heart jumped happily at the little nickname Alexa had given her. She'd always just been Alice. Alice hesitated, her fingers hovering over the buttons on her blouse and then fumbling with the buttons.

"Do you want me to help?" Alexa asked, patiently waiting for Alice to answer.

With more tears, Alice replied, "Yes."

"Yes, *please*," Alexa said, gently stressing the addition. Alice looked at her. There was no malice or anger in her words or face and it made Alice smile.

"Yes, please," Alice repeated, dropping her hands to her side. Alice inhaled a shaky breath, Alexa's light floral perfume mingling with the fruity scent of the bubble bath she had used. Alexa smiled reassuringly at Alice and quickly unbuttoned her blouse, tugging on the edges to free it from her skirt. She carefully folded it and placed it on the counter. Alexa then tucked her thumbs into the elastic of Alice's flower-print, ankle-length skirt and gently tugged it down over her hips. The lacy underwear threw Alexa for a brief moment. It was sensual and matched her bra, the black material contrasting her pale skin. Alexa swallowed, trying to steady her hands. It was the first time she touched Alice's body. Alice stepped out of the skirt, placing her hand on Alexa's shoulders for a little support. She felt goosebumps kiss her skin as the cool air flowed over her from the open doorway. Alexa took in the girl's body. Various colorful tattoos were covering her right arm and several large tropical flowers on her thigh. She made a note to ask her about them later. Right now, Alexa just wanted to get her warm and comfortable and let her be. Alexa reached around her, unclasping her bra. Alice's breasts bobbed free, and Alexa took a moment to admire the perkiness of her small breasts. Alice stepped out of her underwear as well. She hadn't worn her pull-up today. Her brain had been a tired mess when she'd woken up this morning, so she had left just about everything at home.

"I'll wash these for you," Alexa said, carefully placing Alice's things in a neat little pile on the countertop. Alice nodded.

"Hey, love," John called from the bedroom, standing just outside the doorway to afford them some privacy. Alice instinctively covered herself, her face flushing a deep scarlet.

"Yeah?" Alexa answered.

"I've left some things on the bed that Alice can wear for the night. I thought she might like something a little more comfortable to wear."

"What a great idea!" Alexa said. She

turned to Alice. "Are you okay with that?" She nodded.

"Thank you," Alice whispered. Alexa looked at her big, trusting eyes and smiled.

"Anything, Alice. I mean it."

"Why are you so nice to me?" Alice blurted.

"Aren't you weirded out by me? By my voice, by my crying, my neediness, and by me being a little?" Tears rolled down her cheeks. Alexa smiled again, "You needed someone to take care of you, Alie." Alice pouted, "Yeah, but—"

"You're perfect the way you are, Alice. Come. Let's get you cleaned up so you can wear something cute and warm." Alexa smiled, interrupting her.

Alice carefully dipped a foot into the tub, testing the water with her toes. She giggled as the bubbles tickled her foot as she lowered it in.

"How's the water? Do you need me to add some cold in?" Alexa asked.

"No, it's perfect," Alice said.

"Thank you," she added, almost forgetting her manners again. Alice stepped into the tub and lowered herself to the water. The peach scent of the bubble bath enveloped her, and Alice exhaled a pent-up breath. Her tears had finally dried up. The last few weeks of her life had gone completely unhinged.

"I thought you might like this," Alexa said and handed her a rubber duck that was dressed up like a unicorn. Alice giggled again, hastily reaching out to grab it, but then caught herself. Alexa didn't seem to mind her childlike behavior. It seemed to Alice that Alexa approved that she was so relaxed around her and John.

"It's okay, Alie."
Alice gently took the ducky and thanked her, letting it float between a mountain of peach-scented bubbles. Alexa made herself comfortable on the bathroom floor while Alice slowly warmed up, becoming a little more talkative as the bubbles and warm water did their magic.

"Remember to wash between your toes too, Alie," Alexa said as she watched Alice squeeze a dollop of shower gel onto a sponge.

"Yes, Mommy," Alice said.

There was a heartbeat of stillness when Alice's words left her lips. Her eyes grew wide, and she paused, foam dripping from the sponge into the water. She hadn't meant for the word to come out, but it had. Horror washed over her, and she stared, unblinking, at the water.

"Good girl," Alexa said, not missing a beat. She could tell that Alice was used to having to keep her little self hidden away from people around her. She wondered if Alice had ever had a Caregiver - not just some relationship that had a little kindness to it, but a *real* caregiver.

Alice peeked at Alexa from the corner of her eye as she started washing. The woman was relaxed, sitting cross-legged and watching over Alice as she washed and played with the unicorn ducky.

"Mommy?" Alice asked, testing the word again, feeling self-conscious.

"Yes, Alie?"

"Can I have soup for dinner?" Alexa arched a brow.

"Please?" Alice amended, blushing.

"We'll see what we can scrounge up, baby girl." Alice got out of the tub, and Alexa wrapped her in the biggest, fluffiest, and warmest towel she had ever seen or touched in her entire life. She ran her hands over the soft fibers and inhaled the clean scent. Alice felt safe here with them. Out of habit, she had tried to suppress her change into her little space, but Alexa had gently coaxed her out of her shell. Alice stood for Alexa to dry her. Alexa did so carefully, increasingly aware of how soft Alice's skin was. She swallowed, feeling desire flash hotly through her.

"John picked these out just for you," Alexa said as she led Alice back into the master bedroom. This time Alice had a good look around. The colors were muted grays and dark greens, giving the room an ethereal, forest-like feel.

"It's so cute," Alice exclaimed excitedly as she held up the onesie that John had laid out on the bed for her. It had a multitude of colorful cartoon sheep pulling various faces printed all over the black material. Alexa helped her get dressed and gently tied the belt of the robe around her waist, "How's that? Not too tight?"

"No, it's just right, Mommy." Alice was feeling lighter. The warmth from the bubble bath and Alexa's gentleness had soothed her nerves.

"What's your favorite flavor soup, baby girl?" Alexa asked, tucking a stray strand of hair behind Alice's ear.

"Chicken."

"That sounds delicious," Alexa said.

"Let's go see what we can do about making you some soup."

"Okay, Mommy."

Chapter 7

"I thought we could take some time off," Alexa offered the next morning when they were all seated around the kitchen table. Alice was happily eating her Fruit Loops, humming along to a song in her head. She had slept like the dead - better than she had in months. Just the thought that John and Alexa were there had made it possible for Alice to relax and stay in her little space as long as she had wanted. She had feared their disgust, but they had happily accommodated her. Alexa had held her as she fell asleep while she sang to her. Alexa's voice was soothing, deep, and it resonated within her. It hadn't taken long before her heavy lids had dragged themselves shut, and Alice had fallen asleep easily, happily and lightly drifting through the songs.

"When do you want me to take you home, Alie?" Alexa asked. Alice froze, spoon halfway to her mouth, milk dribbling onto the counter. The suddenness of her question had startled Alice.

She hadn't thought of going home. Did they not want her?

Alice swallowed and set the spoon back in the bowl, surreptitiously wiping the drops of milk away with the sleeve of a borrowed robe. She cleared her throat, feeling suddenly exposed.

"Can...Can't I stay here? With you?" Alice asked, her voice still small. She dreaded the thought of having to go home and deal with whatever waited for her there.

"Just for a little bit?" Alice added.

"We thought you'd, well, want to go home," John said, his gaze flicking from Alexa to Alice and back again. He was surprised that Alice had wanted to stay.

"Of course, Alice," Alexa said, "You're welcome to stay as long as you need."

"Really?" Alice asked, fiddling with the sleeves of the robe, pulling at the loose threads nervously. She wanted to stay in her little space just a while longer. She liked being there with them.

"You're not upset with me?" Alice asked,

forcing her lip to stop quivering.

John smiled wide, reflecting the warmth in his eyes, "No, baby girl. You didn't do anything wrong." Alice blinked away the sting of tears and nodded, returning to her Fruit Loops.

"Your clothes are all washed, Alie," Alexa said.

"My clothes?" She blinked in confusion, temporarily forgetting that the robe and onesie were not hers. She glanced at where Alexa had pointed, and a fresh wave of sadness and anger washed over her.

Alice shook her head vigorously, closing her eyes and pursing her lips together. She remembered the boxes that were still waiting for her. Alice's emotions were hot and wild and so very close to the surface the past couple of days that she barely felt the tears roll down her cheeks again.

"Why the tears, sweetheart?" John asked.

"I don't want to wear that." Alice was pointing at her cleaned and freshly pressed work outfit. John looked at Alexa, then back at Alice.

"You don't have to wear it," he said,

smiling gently and patting her hand.

"I don't?"

"No," John said, shaking his head.

"But I can't go out like this," Alice said, still sniffling, looking down at herself. Her heart was breaking. She didn't want to dress like a grownup. She didn't want to wear that stupid blouse. It was too plain, and the skirt was itchy. Alice's breath hitched, and she let out a sob. John wiped her cheeks with both his palms and pulled Alice in for a firm hug.

"I've got something that you can wear, Alie," Alexa said. "Then, when we go out, you can buy yourself something you like." John released her, and Alice looked at Alexa, her lashes wet, and her face already puffy.

"I don't have to wear that?" Alice asked again, pointing at the outfit. Alexa shook her head.

"Come now. No more tears, okay?" John said, wiping at the moist trails on her face. Alice nodded and rubbed her chin on her shoulder. She felt squirmy and uncomfortable.

She was embarrassed at the way she had reacted. Alexa and John had been gracious, letting her wind down and stay over. They had fed her and cared for her, and she had acted like Alice stopped her thought.

"Let's go get ready, Alie," Alexa said, calling her over, holding her hand out for her. Alice hopped off the stool and shuffled over to her, still fiddling with the cuffs of the robe. Her face was warm, and her tears were very close to the surface again.

She peeked up at Alexa and saw no trace of annoyance on her face. Her smile was genuine, and her eyes were welcoming. Alexa led her back to the room she had spent the night in. It had been decorated to accommodate a little, Alice realized. There were plenty of stuffies and other toys decorating the top of the dresser.

"Do you have your own little?" Alice asked, her eyes taking in the room where she had slept in the daylight. Alexa glanced at her. Her hands paused within the depths of the drawer.

"We've had a few, but after a while, we

realized that we were better sharing our love with as many little ones who needed it."

"I had no idea," Alice mumbled, sitting on the bed, examining one of the bear stuffies. It had a little blue bow tie and checkered vest. She smiled and set it back on its spot next to the otter.

"If you want, we can take you to a play party some time," Alexa offered.

"Why?"

Alexa scrunched up her nose and pretended to be very interested in the different pull-ups as she gathered her thoughts.

"You might enjoy spending some time with other littles, or you could even find a Caretaker of your own."

"Oh," Alice said, a little hurt by the implication.

"Oh, here we go," Alexa said and pulled out a lovely muted yellow dress.

"What do you think?"

Alice fell in love with the dress the second she saw it. It had short, puffy sleeves and soft, ribboned frills that accented the neck and hemlines.

"It's beautiful," she crowed. Alexa smiled and held it up to Alice's form.

"I think you'll make all the other little girls jealous, Alie."

Alice giggled and held the dress to her, twirling around as she watched the fabric and frills ripple with the movement.

"Do you want to come to choose a pull-up? I bought a couple of new ones just last week," Alexa said.

Alice, still holding on to the dress, ran to Alexa and peered into the drawer. There, next to the onesies, were fresh stacks of pull-ups. Alexa unpacked them for her, and Alice landed on one that matched her dress.

"This one with the little owls," Alice said.

"Okay, this one it is. Do you want me to help you get dressed today?" Alexa asked as she shut the drawer and stood.

Alice thought for a moment and nodded. The buttons on the back of her dress would require an extra pair of hands to close.

"Alright, baby girl."

***

Alice held Alexa's hand the whole time, even though she had been too excited to stand still for very long. Alexa had allowed herself to be led around by little Alice as she flitted from storefront to storefront.

"Oh, look at this!" Alice crowed and dragged her inside. John patiently followed behind, holding their purchases, laughing at the strange looks their little band was eliciting.

"Alright, last stop," John said when he finally caught up with his girls, "I need food." Alice pouted, "But, Daddy, we're having so much fun."

"Alice," Alexa warned. Alice dropped her head a little and mumbled an apology.

"Don't worry, baby girl. We've got plenty of time the rest of the week to go anywhere we want," John said.

"Can we come back tomorrow?" Alice asked, negotiating. She looked longingly at the furry pink jacket that had caught her eye. Alice made a small mental note that even if Mommy didn't want to get it for her, she'd come back on her own.

"What do you think, love?" John asked, wrapping an arm around his wife's waist, pulling her in for a kiss.

"I suppose we could come back after lunch." Alice's eyes lit up.

"But," Alexa added, "Only if you promise to be a good girl. Only good girls get presents." Alice nodded eagerly, her heart soaring, "I promise I'll be good."

"Good girl," John said and kissed the top of her head, wrapping his free arm around her waist, pulling her tightly to him. He didn't care about the looks he was receiving from patrons. He felt that what anyone did in their free time had zip to do with anyone else.

"What do you want to eat?" John asked as they headed to the food court. As promised, Alice had proven to be an exemplary good little girl. She did still try pushing for a second ice cream cone, but she didn't act out more than that. Alice had held their hands and kept up polite conversation as Alexa and John did some shopping of their own. John had his eye on a brand new Ibanez guitar and played a few bars of the song he was working on to test it. Alice saw the way his eyes lit up, and his entire demeanor changed as soon as he began to play. She glanced at Alexa and saw the deep love she held for him displayed for the world to see.

After some internal debate, John set the guitar back on its stand and spoke to the manager. They exchanged numbers, and John greeted him with a hug and a slap on the back.

"Awesome. Let me know when it comes in."

"What was that?" Alexa asked.

"I may or may not have asked him to let me know the moment a very special girl comes in," John said. Alexa laughed, teasing him.

"A special girl? So you're getting yourself a

brand new baby? What about us?"

Alice watched their exchange in silence, a smile on her lips. They made jokes and poked fun once in a while, but never stepped over boundaries. Alice was a little envious of how at ease they were with each other and how safe they felt together. John shrugged, his face turning a slight shade of pink. She playfully pushed his shoulder.

"Is it the cherry red bass?" His face broke into an unbelievably big grin, "You know me so well."

"Did they find you one?" Alexa gasped, her eyes growing wide as she finally understood his excitement. John was giddy, excitement making his eyes tear up, and he nodded. His voice was thick with emotion, "Fender, 1951. A cherry-red, four-string precision bass."

"That's amazing! After how many years, my love?" Alexa hugged him tightly, his excitement bubbling through her, infecting her.

"Is that a good guitar, Daddy?" Alice asked, wanting to be part of the excitement and conversation.

"My granddaddy used to own one just like it before it got destroyed in a fire."

"Oh, no," Alice clapped her hand over her mouth in shock.

"He taught me how to play, and it's because of him that I make music," John said, love in every crease on his face.

"If you want, I can teach you, too, Alie."

***

"I've been to almost all of your concerts, Daddy," Alice said as she licked melted ice cream from her hand. It was unseasonably warm today, but under the cool shade of the oak trees, it was a pleasant day.

"Oh, that is so cool!" John exclaimed, "Which song is your favorite?" He leaned forward excitedly. Music was his passion and finding someone who enjoyed his music always sent a jolt of happiness through him.

"Double Down."

"Double Down? What about Boo You?"

Alexa hid a smile as she watched the two of them interact. She loved John to the ends of the earth, and Alice was already growing on her. The girl was curious, funny, and seemed to fit in rather well. Alice had taken some time to adjust to them, but Alexa could tell that she was going to be a tough nut to crack.

"What about…" John paused for effect, tapping his finger on his chin, "One More Time?"

"Oh, yes! *That* one is my favorite!" Alice said, rocking back, holding onto her knees.

"Really? That's my favorite, too." John said. Alice giggled, throwing her head back. She was becoming more comfortable with them, and it made Alexa happy. The girl needed someone to take care of her, and she felt that the two of them were exactly what Alice needed.

"You can't have any favorites!" Alice exclaimed.

"Why not?" John gasped in mocked disbelief.

"Because you wrote *all* those songs, Daddy. You have to like them all, or you wouldn't play them." John paused for another moment, pretending to think over her words.

"I don't know..." he muttered, "Some of those songs are kinda stupid."
Alice laughed again, her grin lighting up her eyes and face, highlighting her beautiful soul. When she dropped her guard, Alexa could easily see herself falling in love with her. By the look on John's face, she could tell that he was smitten. Alexa hid a smile behind her plastic cup as she drank the fruit juice. There were few families around them, many preferring to spend the day either indoors or at the waterpark for the heat. They had changed their minds, opting for the park instead. Alexa didn't want to deal with large, unruly crowds today. Spending one on one time with Alice was so much more fulfilling than having her distracted by all the different rides. It was peaceful here in the shade of the large tree. Alexa knew that she wanted Alice as her little. Alice seemed to love John, but she knew it could be some time before the girl was completely comfortable with them. It would be some time

before she would trust them, but Alexa knew she was willing to put in the effort to win Alice's trust.

"What are you thinking?" John leaned over and whispered in her ear while Alice was distracted by a bee that had flown closer to their treats.

Alexa grinned and kissed him, his warm lips, making her tingle. She pulled away.

"I'm thinking about how much I love seeing the two of you together."

"She's got a good heart," John said. Their talk was interrupted when Alice let out a small, panicked squeak. The bee had flown too close to her face, and Alice had instinctively swatted at it. This had upset the bee and made it buzz angrily around her.

"Kill it! Kill it!" Alice shrieked and tried to scoot away from it as fast as possible while flailing her hands over her head, trying to protect her face.

"Hold still, Alie," Alexa said in a firm voice, and she got to her knees to help. She gently ushered the bee away while John made Alice lie down on the blanket and covered her head with her hands. Alexa managed to shoo the bee away and put out a small piece of fruit further away from them in hopes of drawing it that way.

"We don't hurt them, Alie," Alexa said. "It only wanted a little bit of food."

"But it tried to hurt me," Alice whined.

"Only because you tried to hurt it first," John said and helped her sit upright, checking to see if she had any stings.

"Are you hurt?" He asked, trying to draw her attention back to him. Alice was distracted, looking around her for any more bees. When he was satisfied that she was completely unharmed, he kissed the knuckles on both hands and crouched in front of where she sat.

"Come see," John said and held his hand out to her.

"Where are we going?" Alice asked.

"I want to show you that the bees' only attack if they feel threatened." Together they walked to a nearby flower bush and squatted down. Alice was uncomfortable. She didn't like bees.

"But, Daddy!"

"Just watch," John said and poured a little bit of liquid into the lid of his water bottle and held it out to the bees buzzing around the bush. He felt Alice's grip on his arm tighten.

"It's okay, Alie. Just watch."
So she did. At first, nothing happened. Then a couple of bees buzzed around the lid and carefully landed. She watched as their funny little bee tongues touched the water for a few seconds before taking off again. They ignored the two of them, focusing on the water, zipping back and forth between the flowers and their small gift of water.

"I know they can seem scary, but they're just trying to have a good life," John said. He stroked her hair. Alice giggled, enjoying the attention of John and watched the bees wiggle their yellow butts as they landed.

"They do look kinda cute with their small,

fat bodies," Alice said.

"Yeah, they kinda do," John smiled.

***

They slept in late a few days, lazing around the house until mid-afternoon before deciding how they were going to spend their time. Alice had been eager to share her ideas, and while going to the Reptile House for the third time would have made her day, Alexa chose the beach. It was less than a ten-minute walk from their home, and this late in the afternoon, it would be empty. John tickled Alice, and they rolled around on the beach, sand getting in their hair and sticking to their sunscreen-layered skin. It was wonderful to get to know Alice. She was smart and humorous, but her sharp tongue often got her into trouble. They had gone over some rules with her, keeping the list short. Even though Alice hadn't yet shown interest in being with them long-term, it was still important to have rules in place so that they all knew where they stood with one another.

1. *No swearing.*

2. *No running around in public by herself.*

3. *Help with chores.*

Alexa and John felt that, at the very least, having rules in place could help her adjust to the idea of staying with them long-term. Alice hadn't said which way she was leaning as far as becoming a permanent part of their little family, but she did mention next-times and talked in terms of future events. This gave them hope.

John watched the sunset while Alice made crumbly sandcastles next to them. Alice lined her crooked towers with broken seashells and asked Alexa to help take pretty pictures for her Instagram.

Alexa and John would spend each evening in each other's arms, recalling the day and delighting in the pleasure they would have if Alice agreed to be their little.

For the moment, Alice seemed to be content just being herself. She demanded nothing from them and genuinely seemed to enjoy spending time with them.

***

Alice pushed her boundaries with John and Alexa more frequently. She was getting bolder and more confident in herself. When they had asked her to help clean up after dinner, Alice had pouted and refused. While some punishments were put into place, they weren't anywhere near where they could have been. Alexa hadn't wanted to push too hard, and Alice had taken that as a little challenge to see just how much she could get away with.

"Alice, we've talked about this." Alice stomped her foot and stared John down. She didn't want to go to bed. She didn't want to clean. Alice stood firm in her stubbornness. She wasn't tired. She didn't like that she had to be in bed while Mommy and Daddy were awake watching television or doing other things.

"Alice," John said, his voice hard. Alice was pushing their boundaries again, and he wasn't having it this time.

"It's time for bed." Alexa could see the irritation scrunch up his shoulders.

"No."

"Why not?" Alexa asked Alice, placing a calming hand on her husband's arm.

"Because I don't want to."
Alexa gave Alice a stern look.

"Excuse me?"
Alice pouted and lifted her chin in defiance.

"I'm not sleepy. You're still awake, so why can't I be?"

"Growing girls need their sleep, Alie,"
Alexa said patiently.

"No." Alice knew she was being pig-headed, but she was too far along with her stubborn refusal that she felt it would be dishonest to pull back. Alice glared at them, and they matched her stare for stare.
Alexa sighed.

"You're only going to make your punishment worse if you keep going, Alice."
She shook her head.

"Bedroom. Now," John said. Alice's eyes

widened at the anger in his voice. Instinctively, she glanced at his hands and took a step back.

"Alice, go. Please," Alexa said firmly. Alice had gone too far. Finally, she obeyed them and waited in her room for the inevitable.

Alice jumped as the door opened, and Alexa stepped through, a stern, unhappy expression on her face.

"Alie, you know why you were sent to your room, right?" Alexa asked.

Alice nodded.

"Tell me."

"I back talked and didn't do my chores."

"And?"

"I argued."

"Good. Now, let's talk about what you've done." Alexa hated punishing Alice like this, but she had gone too far. Her stubbornness was going to get her into much bigger trouble later on.

"You've been a naughty girl today, Alie," Alexa said.

Alice dropped her gaze to the floor, hanging her

head slightly, "But I'm—"

"Alice. Enough." Alexa cut her off and sat on the edge of the bed.

"I'm sorry, Mommy," Alice said, her voice weak and her legs trembling.

"The rules are there for your health and safety, Alice. We don't say the things we do just because we can and want to."

Alice nodded.

"I know."

"Promise me that you'll try to be a better little girl from now on, okay, baby?"

Alice nodded again.

"Use your words, Alie."

"Yes, Mommy. I promise I'll try harder to be a good little girl."

***

"Alice," John said, calling her over to where he and Alexa were setting the table for dinner. She had taken a break from her little space and was getting ready to face the mountain of stuff she had stuffed into a dark corner of her mind.

"Yeah?" By the end of the week, Alice had been able to relax and process the difficult past few days and had managed to set a plan in motion. Alice would spend some time apart from them while she returned home to deal with her adult responsibilities.

"We want you to be our little."
Alice paused and stared at the two of them over the rim of her coffee cup. Her eyes drifted downwards to the paperwork in his hands.

"I know things have been a little difficult for you, but we love spending time with you, and we want you to be ours."
Alice's heart thumped hard.

"Really?"

"Really," Alexa said. Her heart was clamoring in her chest and attempting a steep climb out of her throat. Alice was the perfect fit for the two of them. She fit in with them so completely that it was difficult to see themselves taking another little, or even worse, seeing her with a different Caregiver.

Of course, if that is what she wanted, Alexa would help Alice find a Caregiver who would make her happy and love and treat her with as much kindness and consistency as she needed. Alexa gripped John's hand so tightly that she could have sworn that she could hear the bones rub against one another, but he did not indicate that it was uncomfortable or painful.

"We will need to review our rules and limits," Alexa added in an attempt to set Alice at ease, "but, yes. We want you to be ours if you'll have us."

"We understand if you don't—"

"Yes."

"What?"

"I said, yes. Yes, I want to be yours."

***

Alice had made herself comfortable on John's lap. She had just woken from a nap, and her hair was wild and unkempt.

"Hi, sleepy-head."

"Hi, Daddy," Alice mumbled and snuggled into his arms. She was warm and comfortable, and felt safe.

"Where's Mommy?" Alice asked.

"She went to shower before dinner." John stroked her hair and gave her a tight squeeze, "Are you hungry?"

Alice nodded.

"Good."

"What are we having?"

"I have no idea. What are you in the mood for?" Alice thought for a moment. "Can we have mac and cheese?"

"Sure," John said.

"But you'll have to help. I don't know how to make it." Alice laughed.

"I'll show you, Daddy."

"Okay, okay."

Alice pressed herself against him. After her punishment last night and sneaking a peek at John and Alexa's alone time, Alice was so worked up that the slightest brush against her body was sending sparks coursing through her. Alice innocently brushed against John's crotch, and another hot spark shot through her, making her instantly wet. He wasn't fully hard, but she could feel the outline of his thick cock through the jeans. Alice licked her lips and straddled John's lap.

Alexa raised an eyebrow as she walked in, towel drying her hair. Alexa was naked under her robe and felt her body tingle at the sight of their little girl straddling her Daddy.

"What are you doing, baby girl?" John asked an amused smile on his face. She wasn't quite as subtle as she thought she was. Alice would have to use her words if she wanted something.

"Nothing," Alice chimed. She slowly, carefully lowered herself onto his lap, feeling his cock through the layers of material.

Alice met Alexa's gaze, and her Mommy nodded.

"Nothing?" John repeated. "Really?"

Alice's cheeks flushed, and she averted her gaze. Alexa was watching them.

"Tell me what you want, Alie. Use your words."

Alice leaned down and whispered into his ear, sensually pressing herself against him, "I want you to play with me, Daddy."

John arched a brow and stifled a smile.

"How do you want me to play with you, baby girl?"

"The way you and Mommy played with each other last night."

"Last night?"

"Yes, Daddy."

John brushed her hair out of her face. The thought of Alice watching him fucking Alexa immediately made him hard, and by the knowing look on her face, she could feel his response.

"So, can we, Daddy?" Alice rolled her hips against him.

"You sure about this, baby girl?" John said.

"You haven't asked for this before."

"Yes, Daddy." When John hesitated, Alice scooted off his lap and reached between her legs.

The clasps on her onesie snapped open. She pulled it up over her head and stood in nothing but her thigh high bunny socks.

John drew in a breath through his teeth.

"Good job, Alie," Alexa said and sat next to him on the couch. John glanced at her.

"Sit on Daddy's lap, baby girl."

Alice obeyed. John's gaze slid over her body, her nipples hardening under his gaze, and her pussy moistening as the rough material of the jeans stroked her clit.

"Rub yourself against him," Alexa said. Alice slowly and rhythmically began rubbing herself against him. Alexa watched, already turned on by this display. Alexa wanted to let Alice do what she wanted, only offering small nudges whenever she noticed her tell-tale moment of uncertainty play across her features. Alice reached between them, unbuttoning his jeans. She slid off his lap and knelt in front of him. His eyebrows shot up.

"Alie, are you sure you want to do this? You know you don't have to do anything you don't want to, right?"

"I know, Daddy. I want to," She reassured him, her small, warm hands wrapped around his cock as she gently coaxed it free from the confines of his boxers and jeans.

Alice licked her lips and took the swollen head of his shaft into her mouth, maintaining eye contact with him as she ever so slowly lowered her head, taking the length of him into her mouth, opening her throat to let him be enveloped. Alice had watched how Alexa had teased and pleased John, and she copied her.

"Good girl," Alexa said, pleased. She bit her lip when she caught sight of Alice's smooth mound, moisture already coating the folds of her pussy lips in a fine sheen.

Alice took her time pleasing her Daddy, listening to his moans and instructions as she sucked on his cock.

"Stop."

Alice pulled back in time, and he panted as he forced his orgasm from peaking. Alice chewed on her bottom lip and then straddled him on the couch, rubbing the head of his cock against her moist pussy lips.

"Fuck me, Daddy," she said.

Chapter 8

"We've come up with some rules that we think you should follow, Alice," Alexa said as they finalized the last bit of the paperwork. Alice pulled the sheet of paper closer and read each one out loud.

"Trust and respect, Mommy and Daddy." Alice looked up at John and Alexa and nodded. It made sense, but she also understood why it had to be in her list of rules.

"Always be on your best behavior, and do your chores." Alice frowned at the thought. She hated doing chores. It was why her small apartment looked like a tornado had gone through it more often than not.

"Eat three meals a day." Alice disagreed and told them so.

"I don't eat that much."

"You've got to stay healthy, Alice. I've seen the way you eat," Alexa said.

"But—"

"That brings us to the next one: no backtalk. We've only got your best interests at heart, so we expect you to listen. Eating three meals a day is not unreasonable. If it's still too much, we can adjust the amount of food."

"Bathe daily." Alice liked to bathe, so that wasn't a rule.

"Don't stay up past your bedtime." Again Alice paused and looked at them. "When is my bedtime?"

"9 PM."

"What?"

"Yes. You have to be well-rested for your job during the week."

"What about weekends? Can I stay up later?"

"We can discuss that." John nodded.

"Don't wander off while we're in public." Alice continued reading from the list, her eyes breezing over all of the notes and changes they had made of the rules and regulations. Alice stopped once in a while to offer an opinion on a certain rule if she felt it was unreasonable. Half the time, Alice got her way. The other half, John and Alexa, had put their foot down when she pushed her luck too far, and she was sent to her room as punishment. If Alice continued, they withheld her orgasms.

They agreed on a safe word, just in case.

"And no going into the naughty store without us."

***

John saw the fear in Alice's eyes and immediately pulled back.

"Hey, baby girl, it's okay." He unlocked the cuffs around her wrists and tossed them aside, rubbing her arms. She had chills.

"Alie, you have to tell Daddy when I'm doing something that scares or hurts you," he said and pulled her onto his lap. He could feel her shaking, and it terrified him.

"Daddy," Alice said after she had calmed down enough to stop her hiccoughs, "I don't like being cuffed."

"We're so sorry, baby," Alexa said and gently stroked her hair. It had come as a surprise to all of them.

Alice had been open to the idea, given that it wouldn't hurt, and it was something she could potentially enjoy. It had been meant to be used as an alternative form of punishment, to be unable to touch either Mommy or Daddy during their sexy playtime. Alice had felt too vulnerable - too scared.

She was starting to develop feelings for her Caregivers, and that made her act out more frequently. Because of this feeling of vulnerability, Alice tested her limits. John and Alexa never lost their cool with her. Alice found this a little annoying, and so she continued to push. When she had gone too far, Alexa sent Alice to bed early.

After an agonizing night of staring at the ceiling, Alice walked into their room in the small hours of the morning and went to their room, sneaking in as quietly as she could.

"Mommy?"

"What's wrong, Alie?" Alexa asked, instantly alert.

"Can I sleep here?" Alice asked, her voice small. She needed some physical contact and didn't know how to ask for it, especially since she was afraid that they would send her away because she had been disobedient.

"Of course, Alie," Alexa said, scooting up to make space for her. She snuggled close to Alexa and whispered, "I'm sorry." Alexa's warm arms wrapped around her, and Alice realized with a start that she was wearing a very thin nightshirt and nothing else. Alice's heart pounded in her ears, and her body broke out in goosebumps. She pressed herself closer to Alexa, inhaling her scent. Alexa felt the girl's body pressed against her, the heat of her skin seeping through the thin fabric of her sleepwear. In the light filtering through the open curtains, Alexa could see her trusting eyes looking up at her.

"Is it okay if I touch you?" Alice

whispered, acutely aware of how her body tingled at every stroke Alexa ran down her back.

Alice let her hands trail down Alexa's body and over her shirt. Her fingers skimmed the hem of her sleepwear and touched the soft flesh of Alexa's thighs.

Alexa's breathing had changed slightly, Alice noted, a thrill of success running through her.

"It's okay, baby girl. You can keep going," Alexa said breathlessly as Alice's fingertips stroked her inner thighs.

Alexa massaged Alice's breasts through her onesie, the fabric unable to hide her hardened nipples.

"I want you to touch me, Alie," Alexa whispered to her little girl.

Alice complied, running her hand up Alexa's leg, pushing beneath the hem of her nightshirt. Her fingers found Alexa's curls, stroking through them, feeling her body heat.

"That's a good girl," Alexa muttered, and she toyed with her nipple, gently tugging on it. A soft moan escaped her lips, and Alice's demeanor changed instantly. Her forwardness had evaporated and was replaced by her submissive demeanor.

"Keep going, little girl," Alexa said as she slowly spread her legs, allowing Alice access to her core.

"Yes, Mommy," Alice said, her face burning and her own body throbbing in response to her fingers sliding into Alexa's moist pussy. Alexa inhaled sharply, biting her lip, pleased by Alice's touch. The girl was a quick study. Alice's fingers massaged her, drawing sighs of pleasure from Alexa.

Alice felt the bed shift behind her.

"You need a hand?" John asked, his voice deep and thick with lust and sleep.

Alice met Alexa's gaze and nodded. She desperately wanted him. Her body burned. A glint in Alexa's eyes spread to a smirk.

"Looks like our little girl can't wait for you to touch her."

"But she's been such a bad girl lately," John said, pressing himself against Alice's ass.

His cock was heavy, having listened to Alexa's moans as Alice touched and pleased her Mommy.

Alice whimpered, "I'll be good, I promise." Her fingers stroked deep into Alexa's pussy, and she moaned loudly and arched her back.

"Promise?" John asked as he ran his hands over Alice's ass, stroking the soft flesh. He reached around, unclipping the clasps of her onesie, purposefully stroking her through the fabric.

"Yes," Alice breathed.

"Yes, who?"

"Yes, Daddy." John continued stroking her cleanly shaven lips, coating his fingers in her moisture.

"Little Alie is already so wet, Mommy," John remarked.

Alice's whole body trembled as she let Alexa and John tease and touch her. The two made turns to stroke her, kiss her, and nibble her exposed skin.

"Please," Alice muttered.

"Please, what, Alie?" John growled in her

ear as he rubbed his cock against her opening.

"Please can I cum?"

Alexa gently bit down on Alice's nipple, running her tongue around the hard nub. The girl moaned and bucked her hips, trying to get the release she desperately craved.

"I think we have punished her enough, don't you?" John asked, reaching over to stroke his wife's pussy lips. She was dripping wet from their play and Alice's fingers, and his cock jerked painfully.

"Please...please."

Her moans were causing cum to leak from the head of his cock as he continued to stroke Alexa.

"Bend over for Daddy," Alexa commanded. Alice obeyed, her mind spinning, and her body thrumming. She got onto her knees and spread her legs for him, stretching her hands out to Alexa. Alexa lay in front of Alice, spreading herself open to her gaze. Without being asked, Alice wrapped her hands around Alexa's hips and pulled her closer. As soon as her tongue touched the soft folds of her lips, she felt

John's hard cock press against her twitching pussy, and a desperate whimper escaped her throat. Alexa chuckled, "Stop teasing our little girl, John. I think she's learned her lesson. Isn't that right, Alie?"

"Yes, Mommy. I promise I'll be a good girl." Alice said, her eyes were glassy from desire and unspent lust. Alexa pulled her closer and kissed her, their tongues dancing as she spread Alice's legs apart, allowing better access for John.

A low, guttural growl started in his throat at the sight of them. Alexa was sensually rubbing their bodies together, their broken, hitched breathing causing his mind to reel. John closed the gap and gripped Alice's hips, interlacing his fingers with his wife's as she held on. He thrust his hardness into Alice's hot, wet pussy. Her body reacted instantly, clamping down on his cock, twitching and pulsing as he pushed deeper inside of her. Alice moaned loudly. All thoughts of behaving fled from her mind. She bucked against him and locked her fingers in Alexa's hair, the other hand finding her core. Alice inserted two fingers into Alexa's pussy, not as gently as she had earlier.

"Fuck," Alexa moaned.

John stroked his cock in and out of Alice's pussy, enjoying the feel of the warmth of her body around him. His breathing was already ragged. The sight of his two beautiful girls giving each other pleasure had pushed him dangerously close to the edge.

Alice moaned into Alexa's mouth and felt her orgasm threaten. She gasped, biting down on Alexa's shoulder, her nails leaving light scratches down her side. She had slipped her fingers out of Alexa's pussy, bracing herself on either side of her body as John thrust wildly into her. Stars burst in front of her vision as soon as Alexa touched her clit with her fingertips. Her scream caught in her throat, her pussy clamped and pulsated around John's thick cock, and Alexa breathed into her ear, sending waves of pleasure and chills rippling over and through her body. Alice had been edging her orgasm for days, and the sudden release made her vision blur, and her whole body convulse and twitch. Her body shook as John fucked her, panting as he came, shooting his cum into her tight pussy.

John continued to thrust into Alice, feeling his cum and her juices leak from her hole, spreading down her thighs to stain the sheets. Her body clamped around him, and he felt a second orgasm build.

"Let me lick you, Mommy," Alice whispered into Alexa's ear. She moved back, exposing herself to Alice's waiting tongue, oblivious to the rising sun lightening the room.

Chapter 9

Alice looked at them, her jaw working and her breathing speeding up. She was utterly overwhelmed by their kindness. It conflicted deeply inside her with what she knew about everyone she had ever come into contact with. David had been oppressive and egotistical about their relationship - demanding and one-sided. Alice had lacked love and kindness from the very people who were sworn to protect and care for her.

Alexa and John shared a look.

"Alice, sweetheart, you need to talk to us." They didn't argue or scream. They only punished her when she was bad and never withheld care. They guided her with love and kindness, and it scared her. They took care of her, and they looked out for her.

Alice wanted so badly to be theirs. She wanted them to love her as much as they loved each other. She wanted to be part of their family. That feeling deep inside her made her uneasy. Still, she couldn't suppress the feeling that they were going to discard her the way her parents had. She couldn't bear losing her Mommy and Daddy. Alice's heart stalled in her chest when she realized that she was beginning to grow attached to them - that she had fallen in love with them.

"I'm going out."

"Alice—"

"I want to go to the mall, and I want to go alone."

Alice had been snarky all afternoon, being as bratty as possible, fighting against any rule they had tried to reinforce, and she all but screamed at them to leave her alone.

Alice had nearly burst into tears when John took her aside and just hugged her. She had pushed him away, rejecting his touch, but he didn't object. He only smiled at her and said, "It'll be okay kiddo." No lecture, no fights - just a hug. He called her for dinner later that night, and Alexa had drawn a bath for her before bedtime.

They didn't treat her any differently. Alexa asked her about her day and allowed her to watch whatever she had wanted.

When it came time for bed, Alexa had gotten her room ready and even had Beanie waiting for her under the covers, tucked in as if he was asleep.

Alice didn't acknowledge or thank them. She glared at Beanie. She glared at Alexa when she said goodnight.

Alice fell into a restless sleep, her nightmares turning their kindness into manipulation and abuse.

The next morning, Alice approached Alexa before breakfast. She had hoped to speak to her before John woke up, but when she got there, he was already brewing a fresh pot of coffee for them.

"Alexa," Alice said quietly. "I..."

Alexa gave her a moment to think, but when it became clear that she wasn't going to say anymore, she spoke, "You know you are free to go whenever you want, Alice."

The words struck Alice with force she didn't

expect. It was what she wanted, but why did Alexa's words hurt so much.

Alice clenched her fists.

"I'll leave then."

"That's not what we're saying, Alice," John said, trying not to make her any more uncomfortable than she already was.

Alice looked at him.

"You're not kicking me out?"

"Of course not, Alie," Alexa said, smiling gently.

"We love having you here."

"Then why did you say that?"

"We want you to know that you're not stuck here. We would never dream of forcing you to do anything you didn't want to do," Alexa said.

Alice's lip quivered. Her emotions were confusing to her. She was scared of how happy she had been over the last week, and it wasn't just the sex.

They were taking care of her, making her lunch, and cooking her favorite meals. And they were letting her be in her little space as long as she wanted. They gently reminded her of the rules and afforded the appropriate punishment, but they never overstepped the boundaries she had put in place. She stomped her foot and walked away, slamming her bedroom door behind her. Alice threw herself onto the floor, kicking her legs in the air, screaming into her pillow. She was shaking, her head hurt, and she desperately wanted them to fight back.

She wanted a reason to leave, but they were kind and understanding. Alice's mind drifted to her parents. She had been forced to leave or get drawn into their shitty lifestyle.

She had been alone even before she had left. Alice didn't know how to behave, especially not when John and Alexa were perfect. Again, Alice avoided them and spent a night thrashing and wishing for dawn.

When dawn finally broke, Alice was staring at the ceiling of her bedroom. Alice sighed. She was torn, the tension causing her stomach to cramp and her muscles to ache from keeping them bunched up.

She chose to have a shower. It was time to make a grown-up decision, and she had run from her troubles long enough.

Alice poured herself coffee from the pot as soon as it was done brewing. This was part of Alexa's routine, Alice had learned. It was nice not to have to struggle with the machine so early in the morning. There was a cold nip in the air when Alice stepped outside, closing their front door behind her.

She was going to take an Uber back to her place. She ignored the frantic texts from Alexa and John until the Uber stopped outside her apartment block.

I'm safe. She texted her reply and set her phone to silent.

She would need to sort her thoughts out before she returned to them.

***

"I don't want to move in," Alice said

finally.

"Okay," Alexa said, waiting for Alice to continue.

"I—" Alice's throat closed up, and she tried to clear it unsuccessfully, "I like having my place."

"I like knowing that I'm not dependent on anyone," Alice added.

"Alie, honey? It's okay to need people and it's okay to want your own space. It doesn't have to always one extreme or the next," Alexa explained.

Alice shook her head. She agreed, but she was trying to keep from freaking out again. She cleared her throat again.

"I don't want to move in."

"We know, honey," John replied.

"You don't have to," Alexa said.

"But I still want to visit. I still want you to be my Mommy and Daddy," Alice quickly added.

"Would you like to set up a schedule?" John suggested. Alice nodded. She needed her place. It was *hers*. She had busted her ass to afford it and then busted her ass to clean it and make it liveable. She felt safe there.

"I'm going to go for a walk, and when I come back, we can talk," Alice said.
John and Alexa let her go, affording her the space she had asked for.
Alice had walked up and down the beach until the sun had set, and a cool wind tugged at her sweater. Alice had finally made up her mind and trudged through the sand back to the house.

"Alexa? John?" Alice asked, drawing their attention away from the television. She closed the distance between them and sat down at the end of the single-seater, facing them. They looked at her, taking in the atmosphere, and they sat up in their seats.

"I need to explain some things."
Alice saw the trepidation on Alexa's face and had to stop herself from aborting her plan and just letting it be.

"Go ahead," John said.

"I grew up in a weird place," Alice said haltingly. She had never told anyone about her past, at least not the way she was planning on telling them now. This was a bare-all, no-holds-barred kind of conversation and one she had been dreading, but here they were.

"I'm going to tell you everything, and I know it could get weird and dark, but I need you to understand certain things about me, and if you think it's something you can't deal with, then I understand." Alice rushed, trying to utter the words before she chickened out.

"But it's something I need to share, or..." Alice stopped short, already feeling the tears threaten to fall. "I feel that you need to know."

"Go ahead, Alice. We promise to listen before making a decision," John said, holding his wife's hand tightly. Alice clasped her hands together and shoved and pinned them between her knees.

"Okay."

She swallowed and started talking, barely hearing her own words over the rushing blood in her ears. She explained everything - what life was like with her parents, the day she left, the messes

she got into, and how it had taken so much time
and energy to drag her ass back out.

"I don't get close to people," Alice said.
"They are unpredictable, and I don't know how
to deal with being happy. Happy. For the first
time since I was three, maybe." Alice saw a glitter
of something in Alexa's eyes before she turned
her head away.

"So the attitude, the fights, everything—"
John was interrupted.

"The bratty attitude, the..." Alice paused,
staring at the ceiling.

"I was scared, and I don't know how to
deal with this." Alice waved her hands around,
indicating she was speaking of everything, and
she looked back at the two of them.

"I don't know how to accept that someone
is willing to take care of me."

"I'm sorry that you had to go through
that," John said.

"I'm not okay with it," Alice said, "Not yet,
but I will be."

"What about other family?" John asked,

aware of his wife's shaking. She had a soft heart, and loving this girl was making the risk of losing her nearly too great to accept.

"They disowned us. My mom stole from everyone and…" Alice looked at the way Alexa was turned away and thought that this was it. This was the moment Alexa would ask her to leave. She was broken, and Alice was giving them every reason to ask her to leave.

"I'm telling you, so you know everything. I'm not good, and you deserve a little that can make you happy," Alice said.
Alexa stood and walked to the kitchen.

"I didn't…" Alice's eyes were wide. She was tense, waiting for the shoe to drop.

"It's okay," Alexa said, smiling. The glittering Alice had seen tears. She had gone to fetch a paper towel to wipe away the smeared mascara.

"It is?" Her voice was shaking now.

"We still want you, Alice," Alexa said. "Your past doesn't define you."

"Yeah, but it's still playing a lead role in

the mess in my head," Alice said. She closed her eyes and rubbed her hands over her face to psych herself up. She wasn't done.

Alice explained the circumstances of her leaving home and those surrounding her parent's death. When she was finished, Alice cleared her throat and looked at each of them in turn.

"I'm sorry for the way I acted," Alice said.

Alexa opened her mouth to reply, but Alice shook her head.

"I mean it. I was a right ass to both of you, and I still can't figure out why you didn't just throw me out."

Alexa smiled warmly, "Alie, we like having you here. We want you to be ours, and everything that comes with it. You're not difficult, but just going through some stuff."

"How could we possibly think of throwing you away, Alice?" John said, putting an arm around her shoulders, squeezing gently.

"Just...talk to us, okay?"

Alice looked at him, tears welling up again. She hated that she was so emotional. Alexa and John made her feel safe to be herself, and it completely unsettled her, but the kindness they radiated made her want to stay and be part of their family so much that she felt it like a physical ache in her chest.

"I'm trying," Alice said, returning their smiles.

***

"You can still stay here as long as you need," Alexa offered. Alice had noticed that she was acting differently. Less warm and less like herself. Alice supposed it was to give her the space she had wanted.

"Are you mad at me?" Alice asked, drinking the tea Alexa had made for them. John had a rehearsal session, so it was just the two of them.

Alexa turned to face her, taking a moment to absorb the girl sitting across from her at the breakfast nook.

"I'm not mad at you, Alice. You're your

own person, and if you felt that we were pushing too hard, all you had to do was tell us."

Alice looked down at her cup.

"We want you to be happy here, and if we're not doing that—"

"I am happy."

"What?"

"I said that I am happy," Alice repeated.

"You and John are amazing. I've never felt safer than I do with you two." She paused.

"It's why—"

"I know," Alexa said. "You don't need to explain it again."

"But I do," Alice said, her voice rising an octave or two. She felt bad for treating them the way she had.

"I was such a brat."

"You were hurting and confused is all," Alexa said.

"Please, just listen," Alexa repeated.

"You have no obligation here, Alice. Truly. If you want to go, you can go, but give yourself a chance at finding true happiness."

Alexa smiled and patted her hand, pouring them more tea while they listened to the ocean.

It was a little awkward at first after she had poured her soul out to them. She hadn't known how to act, and Alice felt a little out of place, wandering around the house. John had returned from rehearsals, and after calling for Chinese takeout, he got comfortable with Alexa on the couch. Alice had isolated herself to the playroom, which was technically her bedroom now, Alice thought, and she carefully straightened and neatened everything that wasn't nailed down. She had worried about their reaction, but there had been nothing for her to be worried about. They had been concerned, appalled, and completely horrid, as they should have been, but not once did they pass judgment on her, her choices, or those of her family's. Alice took some time to accept the fact that both John and Alexa had wanted her. She changed into her pajamas and finally left to join them.
John heard her approach.

"Come here, baby girl," John said, patting the couch beside him. Alexa had wrapped her arms around John and buried her face in the crook of his shoulder while they were watching some romantic movie on Netflix.

Alice watched the two of them together and made the second hardest decision of her life. She walked over to them and sat next to them. She watched the movie with them, eventually putting her head on Alexa's lap, her fingers running through her hair, washing away the rest of her unease.

"Thank you," Alice whispered, and eventually, she fell asleep on her lap, happy and content.

Chapter 10

Alice ended up spending a lot more of her free time with Alexa and John. Alexa and John had given her time and space to process, even when she became unmanageable.

After Alice had thrown her spoon across the room and stormed off, she had come back to clean up her mess to find that they had already done it.

"I..." Alice stammered and stopped talking, wringing her hands together. She was still adjusting to expressing herself in non-destructive ways. Alice had to fight her urge to run away whenever she felt tight bands of anxiety encircle her chest.

Alice chewed on her lip for a moment and then typed something on her phone. Alexa was about to place a hand on her to get her attention, but she stopped when John shook his head.

"We've got this," John said, kissing the back of his wife's hand.

She showed what she typed.

Thank you for trying to understand. Followed by, *I'm sorry.*

"It's okay, baby girl," John said, "It's good that you're talking about things that upset you."

"I'm not used to all these feelings," Alice admitted.

John and Alexa waited. After a while, watching her struggle with getting the right words, Alexa gave her a soft hug.

"Take your time, Alice."

Alice inhaled deeply through her nose and let it out through her mouth in a rush. She started typing on her phone again, pacing up and down, and a little quirk she had picked up from Alexa whenever she was on the phone, stamping out fires.

I like you, and I still want to be your little girl

Alice observed their faces, expecting to see the characteristic masking that her parents had often utilized in front of visitors and other people. The walls never went up, but their reactions still surprised her. John and Alexa both threw their arms around her in a tight group hug, planting kisses on her eyes, cheeks, nose, and anywhere they could reach. Alice giggled and squirmed.

"That tickles!"

"Does that mean you want me, too?" Alice asked.

"Of course!" They said in unison.

"You are so very special, Alie," Alexa said, still hugging her nearly too tightly (though Alice didn't mind). Together they worked on helping Alice express herself, especially when she felt overwhelmed. It happened more often than not where Alexa or John would sit with her in a quiet area in the house and do breathing exercises with her after Alice had shut down on them. They had found a pretty cool app that allowed her to select an emoji or self-uploaded face that corresponded with a mood or feeling, and they worked up from there.

"I'm scared," Alice admitted again later that day.

"What are you scared of?" John asked, sitting across from her.

"That you and Alexa will get tired of me," Alice said. Her eyes were closed, and she was following John's breath, breathing in and breathing out in time with his rhythm.

"It feels surreal," Alice added.

"I understand."

They breathed in the silence. Alice was finally able to get her fight or flight response under control. The rushing of blood and anger in her ears no longer so loud. She wanted John and Alexa to be proud of her, so she tried her hardest.

"Alice, you should know that if you *do* want to leave, we'll help you find someone you'd be happy with."

Alice stifled the panic. Her knee-jerk reaction was to withdraw and question the meaning behind his words. It took a long moment before she was able to speak again without letting her emotions strangle her words.

"I don't want anyone else."

John was quiet for a moment, and Alice opened her eyes to look at him. He was watching her, a crooked smile on his face, and his eyes twinkling.

"What?" She asked.

"It makes me very happy to hear that, Alie."

"Really?"

"Really. Please trust that when we say we want you here, we mean it."

Alice's eyes burned, and she closed them, trying to calm her racing heart, but she couldn't stop herself from smiling.

"How do you feel?" John asked when the timer announced their session was over.

"Happy." Alice embraced it, and even though right beneath the happiness she was scared, she was starting to hope.

She had pulled a few of her usual stunts after that, throwing tantrums and acting like a complete brat on occasion, but eventually, Alice had fallen into her new routine. She even offered to make dinner (with supervision, of course). Alice had been worried that the damage she had done would be irreversible, but those worries had held no water. John and Alexa had carefully nurtured her and, when needed, they had punished her for breaking the rules. Yet they never hurt her or made her feel weird about being herself.

And if things got too tough, Alice could retreat to her room knowing she would be safe. Alexa had suggested that her room was for Daddy and Mommy time only. Even so, there was never any expectation other than being a good girl and following the rules. They respected her space.

***

"I have a new toy I want to try out, Mommy," Alice whispered, her face burning red hot. Curious, John cocked his head and watched as she shifted from one foot to the next, her hands behind her back.

"What is it, Alie?"

Very slowly and very carefully, Alice pulled a black cloth bag from behind her back. Her face burned hotter, and she didn't make eye contact with him. She blushed more and then looked at Alexa.

"I want to show Mommy first."

Alexa caught her meaning and raised her brows at John.

"Oooh, I'm very intrigued."

"Fine," John said dramatically, throwing his head back on the couch. Alice and Alexa laughed and went into the other room.

Alice closed the door behind her.

"What is it, Alie?"

Alice pressed her ear to the door to make sure that John hadn't decided to eavesdrop on them. She wanted to surprise him.

Alexa had an amused smile on her lips, watching her little girl act so secretively. When Alice was satisfied that John wasn't going to spy on them, she opened the wrapping and showed her.

"I thought you and Daddy might like it," Alice said, her ears burning. She had never been one to play outside of her very limited comfort zone, but she wanted to try something that would both surprise and delight them.

Alexa held the item up for inspection. The fur on the tail was soft and full, attached to a small silicone butt plug. Alexa admired how well the tail had been attached to the plug.

"It is so pretty, baby girl. Did you pick it out yourself?"

"The lady at the store said that the silicone was better because I hadn't done this before," Alice said, feeling a little awkward.

Alexa arched a brow.

"You went into the naughty store by yourself?"

Alice flushed her heart racing. She had forgotten about that one rule. Whoops. She averted her gaze and nervously chewed on the inside of her cheek. She crossed her arms in front of her and shifted her weight, her body already tingling under Alexa's gaze.

"You broke a rule, baby girl."

"It was supposed to be a surprise." The words rushed out, "I wanted to go find something we could enjoy together."

She held her breath. Alexa considered the situation for a moment and smiled, "Okay, but just this once. If you want to go to the naughty store again, tell Daddy or me." Alice nodded in earnest.

"I promise."

"Good girl."

Alexa instructed Alice to strip down and get on the bed.

"You ready, baby girl?"

"Yes, Mommy."

"Spread your thighs for me," Alexa said, shaking a bottle of lube as she admired the sight of Alice on their bed, naked, spreading herself open with her hands.

"Is this okay?"

"Scoot up just a bit. I don't want you to fall off the edge, Alie."

There was a tense moment of anticipation, and Alice squirmed as the cold gel dripped on her asshole. Alexa's fingers were hot against her skin as she massaged the lubricant around the entrance. The lubricant warmed up quickly. Alexa continued massaging and added more gel as was needed.

"Relax, baby girl," Alexa whispered,

applying pressure. Alice inhaled sharply, and instinctively pulled away. Alexa simply continued the process: massage, then a bit of pressure. After a short while, Alice opened up to the sensation, actively pressing back against Alexa's fingers. Alexa inserted her well-lubricated finger into Alice's ass hole, and with her free hand, gently stroked over her pussy lips. Alice shivered. Alexa could feel when Alice relaxed enough for her to continue stroking, carefully applying pressure, and stretching Alice out. When Alice's body began quivering, Alexa added a second, well-lubricated finger. Alice's breathing had become shallow and short.

"Good girl, Alie." Alexa slowly pulled away from Alice and added a generous coating of gel to the silicone plug, careful to miss the fur.

"Remember to try and relax, okay?" Alexa asked, pressing the head of the plug against her ass hole, meeting resistance. Alice whined and bit into the pillow.

"Let me know if I should stop, baby, okay?" Alexa said.

"Keep going." Alice was panting, forcing herself to relax as Alexa rubbed more lubricant onto her hole. Pressure caused her eyes to water, but a fresh rush of arousal flushed through her system the moment Alexa pushed the head of the plug in. Alice's eyes rolled into the back of her head, and she panted as her body relaxed around the butt plug.

"Good girl, Alie," Alexa whispered and stroked Alice's ass. Her panties were clinging to her pussy lips, damp from her arousal. Alice's soft grunts of pleasure had set her core burning hotter than she had been in days.

"You ready to show Daddy?"
Alice exhaled shakily, her face flushed as she sat up.

"It feels weird."

"Does it hurt?"

"Not anymore." Alice smiled.

"Maybe I can help make it feel less weird." Alexa offered. Alice recognized the glint in her eyes and licked her lips. Alice nodded.
Alexa moved to sit in front of Alice.

Alice was sitting on her knees, legs slightly apart as she adjusted to the fullness in her ass. She had changed into a cute little nightdress while Alexa had washed lubrication from her hands. It was soft to the touch and clung to her curves. The tail of the butt plug peeked out beneath it. Alice had her hands braced beside her, gently moving her body, accepting the intrusion. Alexa reached between Alice's legs, never breaking eye contact with her, lightly stroking the skin on her thighs as she did so.

Alice bit her lip and subtly spread her legs apart, allowing her Mommy access to the parts of her that were begging to be touched. When Alexa's fingers touched the smooth skin of her outer lips, a smile spread over her face.

"You're already wet, baby."

Alice nodded, blushing furiously. Alexa's openness and gentle voice made her feel less self-conscious. Alexa slipped her fingers between the folds, playing with her clit, watching Alice's facial expression change as her Mommy touched her so intimately. Her little girl quivered, opening her legs wider for Alexa as she pushed her fingers into her. Alexa brought her fingers to her lips, licking Alice's juices from them, sucking on them. Alice's breathing hitched, her body hot and heavy, her eyes locked on Alexa.

"Let's go show Daddy your surprise."

"Do you think he'll like it, Mommy?" Alice asked.

"I think he'll love it so much he would ask you to wear it for him every night," Alexa said.

"Do I look okay?"

"You're so beautiful, Alie."

"Should I change my hair?"

Alexa ran her hands through her hair, and an idea struck her. She hurriedly went searching for some small ribbons she had lying around.

"There we go." Alexa smiled.

"Now, your outfit is complete."

Alice shakily got to her feet, holding on to Alexa's offered hand.

Alexa's fingers had masterfully manipulated her body to the edge before she stopped, causing Alice to be unsteady on her feet. She walked hand-in-hand with Alexa back to where John was waiting as he worked on what Alice and Alexa assumed to be lyrics for a new song.

"Daddy?" Alice said softly.

"You two were gone a pretty long time." He looked up from his notepad, and his jaw dropped. Alexa had carefully tied Alice's hair up into two space buns with bright pink ribbons to match her nightdress. The cotton fabric was light, and John could make out the dark areolas of her nipples, already stiff. His gaze drifted further down, resting at the top of her thighs where the dress ended. The light skin contrasted brightly against the deep color of the fabric. His cock strained against his jeans.

"Turn around so you can show Daddy," Alexa prompted. There was a light to her eyes that John recognized whenever she felt particularly mischievous.

"What are you up to?" His words were barely out when Alice did a little twirl. The gray fur of the tail wrapped gently around her leg and swayed behind her when she came to a stop, facing him.

"Slowly," Alexa said, her eyes locked on her husband.

"Okay," Alice said, feeling more and more comfortable as she moved with the butt plug in. She particularly liked the feel of the soft fur on her thighs.

Alice turned slowly, tiptoeing around, pausing with her back to him. Alice giggled, excitement making her wiggle her butt from side to side. That was precisely what Alexa had been waiting for. Her smirk had turned into a grin, and she held Alice in place.

"What do you think, Daddy?" Alice asked, peering over her shoulder at him.

"Wiggle your tail for Daddy, Alie," Alexa prompted.

Alice obliged, delighting in the sounds of barely-controlled desire coming from behind her. Alice looked at Alexa through her lashes; her bottom lip still caught between her teeth.

"Can I do another twirl?"

"Of course, baby girl," John replied. Alice

grinned happily and twirled again, faster this time, giggling as the tail swished around her legs. She twirled around again, the hem of her dress rising with her arms. John clenched his teeth and sat forward in his seat. The way Alice's hair had been tied up made her look perfectly wolf-like. Her eyes were big, glittering with excitement, and her smile was infectious. John made to reach for Alice, but Alexa stopped him, a grin on her face and a devious glint in her eyes.

"No, no. Not yet."

"Why?" John breathed and pressed the palm of his hand against his groin as he leaned back in an attempt to lessen the discomfort.

"You'll get your turn. It's Mommy's turn now," Alexa said and began unbuttoning her blouse.

John's eyes grew wide.

"You're evil. You know that?" He was grinning but growled through his teeth at her. Alexa was going to tease him within an inch of his life. His cock was already throbbing against

the zipper, his jeans becoming more and more
uncomfortable as he watched Alice do another
small twirl before Alexa went to stand behind
her.

"Yes, Daddy, it's Mommy's turn." Alice
giggled.

Alice gently tugged on the hem of Alexa's robe,
exposing her pussy to his gaze. Even in the dim
light, he could make out the moisture that coated
them and her thighs. She was already wet and
waiting. His cock jerked. Alexa stroked Alice as
she kept her eyes on John. He rubbed himself
through his jeans.

"No touching," Alexa said.

"Yeah, Daddy, no touching," Alice
repeated and giggled. Her humor was cut short
as Alexa delved between the folds, searching for
her core, her fingers still drawing hot trails over
her skin. John balled his fists behind his head,
his willpower waning as he watched his wife
finger Alice. The girl had her head thrown back,
her eyes closed, and her legs were buckling. She
was small enough that Alexa had no trouble

supporting her weight. She lifted Alice's leg,
exposing her core to John's gaze, where her
fingers were rhythmically pushing in and out.
Alice's breath hitched, and Alexa pulled back.

"Not yet, Alie."

Alice protested and pressed herself against
Alexa, her nails digging into Alexa's forearm.

"You don't want me to withhold your
pleasure entirely, do you?" Alexa warned.

"Bad girls don't get to have release."

Alice shook her head.

"I'm sorry, Mommy."

Alice removed her nightdress as her Mommy had
instructed and blushed as she caught John
openly staring at her. Her gaze dropped to his
lap, where his bulge was obvious, and she licked
her lips. Alexa put on a little show for her
husband. She could see the muscles in his jaw,
working as he fought to control himself. She
twirled around, suckled on Alice's nipples, and
had her help Alexa undress. She enjoyed the
sensation of Alice's short nails scraping over her
skin as she undid the buttons on Alexa's blouse.

Without being prompted, Alice lowered her head to Alexa's nipple and pulled the stiff little nub into her mouth. The sudden sensation spread chills over her body, making her tingle with anticipation. Alice felt Alexa's hands on the back of her head, gently holding onto her as her tongue flicked over her nipple. With her free hand, she massaged Alexa's other breast, her fingertip tracing the outline of her areola, drawing spirals until she flicked gently over the tip. Alice repeated the motion in the opposite direction as she tugged on Alexa's nipple with her teeth, flicking her tongue back and forth over the sensitive nub. Alexa lay down on the carpet and beckoned Alice over, spreading her legs wide. She dropped to her knees next to her.

"John?" Alexa asked.

"Would you like some help with that?" She licked her lips and looked pointedly at his crotch. The dark look of desire in her gaze made him groan out loud.

"Fuck, yes," John said and stood. His hands immediately went to his fly and popped the button. The heaviness of his cock pressing against the zipper made it slide down an inch before stopping. Alice's eyes followed the dusting of dark hairs peeing from beneath the shirt down behind the zipper of his jeans.

"Help, Daddy, Alice." Alexa's voice was dripping with lust, her fingers quickly bringing her close to an orgasm as she watched John take a step toward them.

John paused in front of Alice, his cock jerking, making the teeth of the zipper slip apart ever so slightly. Having Alice kneel in front of him like this was driving him insane. The tail seemed to naturally follow the curve of her body and match the movement of every shift. He was mesmerized by little Alice. When her hand reached up and touched the metal tab of the zipper, his cock jerked, and he felt cum bead and trickle slowly over the head. Alice knew from experience just how big John's cock was. She fantasized about having him inside her whenever she was spending the week alone at her place. Yet, she couldn't help her eagerness in freeing him or the excitement she felt when she finally held him in her hands. She wiped at a drop of cum and licked it from the pad of her finger.

"Take Daddy's cock into your mouth, baby girl," Alexa whispered, watching as his cock pulsed in anticipation. Her body twitched as she came closer and closer to finishing herself off. Alice took John as deep as it could go, his girth filling up her small mouth. John grabbed her head and laced his fingers through the hair, taking hold of her, controlling the depth and speed of his thrusts, impatient with how torturously slow Alice was taking things. She looked up at him from beneath her lashes and resisted, that same mischievous glint in her eye that Alexa had had. Reluctantly, he released her and stood back, panting.

"Baby girl." His voice was pleading, cum drops appearing after each small spasm of his cock.

"Not yet, Daddy," Alice said, complying Alexa's words. Alexa had planned to ride John's cock as she came, but the thought was shattered when Alice scooted closer. She reached over to her, running her hand against the soft inner skin of her thigh. Her fingers trailed up, searching. As Alice's fingers made contact with her mound, she arched her back, all plans of taking it slowly dissolving with each soft stroke. Alice ran her hand over her mound, the short hair tickling her palm. Alice circled her thumb over Alexa's clit. Her Mommy moaned, and Alice smiled, "Am I doing okay?"

"Perfect, baby girl," Alexa said, enjoying the attention of her little girl. Alice ran her tongue over Alexa's clit, tasting her juices. Alice sat up, her fingers returning to Alexa's pussy, pushing two fingers into her moist depths. She leaned over and pulled a nipple into her mouth, rhythmically pumping her fingers into Alexa's pussy, feeling her body twitch around them. Alexa moaned.

"Keep going, baby girl, just like that." Alice fingered her, keeping her pace steady, gently tugging on her nipple with her teeth, suckling on it.

"You're such a good girl. You're doing so well," Alexa said, her head leaned back against the floor and her arms reaching for purchase. Alice's heart rose. She liked being called a good girl. It sent a tingle through her body, and her pussy twitched as she thought about how happy Alexa sounded.

"Keep going, baby girl," Alexa encouraged her. She glanced at John, his cock hanging out of his jeans, thick and heavy. The head glistened, and his cock twitched as he watched them. Alice slowed down slightly, eliciting a sound of frustration from Alexa.

"Alie."

She brought her tongue to Alexa's swollen lips, delving between the folds, finding the delicate button that would push Alexa over the edge.

"Oh, fuck."

Alice sped up her thrusts, curling her fingers slightly, stroking the inner, ribbed walls of Alexa's tight pussy. She shuddered and grunted in response to Alice's tongue and fingers working her closer to her climax. John took his painfully hard cock into his hand and squeezed it lightly a few times. He was attempting to stave off the orgasm he could feel dangerously close to the surface. He wrapped his fingers around his shaft tightly this time, pinching the head of his cock between his thumb and finger.

Alexa cursed as she came.

"On the floor, Daddy," Alice said, giggling, her fingers still working in and out of Alexa's pussy. Dazed and holding on by sheer willpower, John obeyed her, his eyes never leaving her face. Alice licked her lips again, her heart beating furiously, encouraged by John's obvious arousal and by Alexa's soft sighs of pleasure as she came down from her orgasm.

She carefully tugged the waistband of his jeans down over his hips, fully freeing his cock. Alice trailed her fingertips down his legs as she slid his jeans to his knees. She stood over him, straddling him, a grin on her face.

"Can I sit on your lap, Daddy?" Alice asked with feigned innocence, swirling her fingers over her clit, sending sparks of heat through her.

John could only nod and watch as she lowered herself to her knees, slowly impaling herself on his cock. The joy on her face nearly broke him, but he grasped the leg of the coffee table, his knuckles turning white from the force of it. Alice slowly rocked herself against him, forcing his thick shaft deeper into her pussy. Alexa crawled over to them and kissed him deeply as Alice rode him.

Strands of her pink hair had escaped from their buns and were now tickling her neck and back as she threw her head back, savoring the tightness of having both her holes filled.

"Can I make Daddy cum yet?" Alice asked, her body hot and throbbing.

"Not yet," Alexa said with a giggle.

"I think you should get off and come here."

Alice obeyed, his cock springing free as she went to where Alexa had pointed. She had changed places with her, Alexa now straddling John in the same way she had.

"Touch yourself for Daddy," Alexa whispered breathlessly as she lowered herself onto John's cock. She moaned sensually and gyrated her hips, eliciting an answering moan from him. Alice spread herself open to his gaze, her fingers finding her soft folds, running her fingers through her juices.

"Good girl," John muttered. He clasped his hands together behind his head, fighting the urge to touch either of them. Alexa lifted herself away from him, his cock pulling free, pulsing once, and bigger drops of pre-cum dribbling down his shaft.

Alexa took his cock into her mouth, tasting herself on him, mixing with his pre-cum. His cock jerked in her mouth, and his balls tightened. John panted and growled, holding on to his sanity by the skin of his teeth. Alexa knew exactly how to break him, and she enjoyed every minute of it. He watched as Alice inserted first one finger, then another, into her pussy. She was sitting too close to him. All he had to do was reach out, and he would be able to touch her.

One soft pull and she would be close enough for his touch to do what he had wanted since she had walked into the room. One soft pull and he could put his lips to her dripping wet pussy, lick her soft folds, and suckle on her swollen clit. Alice saw the lust in his eyes, and a thrill went through her. It was a different dynamic this time. Alexa had wanted to tease John, and Alice could tell that he had loved every torturous moment of it. While she had been a little reluctant at first, seeing the smile on his face and the gaze that could devour her, Alice had grown more comfortable in her role as a seductress. Denying him made him fuck harder, it made him more desperate, and Alexa loved that about him. She wanted Alice to experience that same side to him. She wanted her to experience John's cock when there were no barriers and no caution. Alice fingered herself, stroking her clit in just the right way to edge her closer to an orgasm. Her whole body trembled, and she breathed hard.

"Don't cum yet, Alie," Alexa said as she lowered herself onto John's cock again. Hot and thick, he filled her, stretching her pussy walls as she stroked him. She could feel the heat of his thick shaft, warming her from the inside. His cock twitched, and his balls tightened. Reluctantly, Alexa pulled back again. The tortured expression on his face was delicious, and she straddled his thigh, running her nails over his sac.

Alice pulled her fingers away as her pussy twitched. She had come so close. Alice made eye contact with John and grinned, a naughty idea popping into her head. She suckled on her fingers, watching his jaw clench. Alice leaned closer to John and kissed him, the taste of her moisture and desire clinging to her tongue. Alexa felt his whole body stiffen beneath her. John was reaching his breaking point. She lowered herself down on his cock a final time, and the veins in his neck distended as he struggled with his self-control.

"Alexa, fuck. No, I'm..." His words were strangled, and he thrust his hips, groaning, and no longer in control of himself. John didn't allow her to pull away this time, his hands holding her in place. He thrust into her hard and fast, watching her breasts bounce and her eyes close as she derived pleasure from his roughness, Alice's scent still in his nose, and her taste still on his lips. He felt his climax build. His cock was hot and heavy. Alexa's body clamped around him, milking him, tightening as she matched his rhythm. When she came again, Alexa threw her head back, a growl stuck in her throat, her nails digging into the skin of his thighs as she held him in place. Her pussy clamped around his cock. John gripped her hips tighter and increased his speed. He followed her soon after. His orgasm tore through him with so much force that he went dizzy from it. Alexa exhaled a shaky breath and lay on top of him; his cock still twitching inside her pussy. She kissed his neck and giggled happily. Alexa rolled off of him, panting, grinning, and running her fingernails lightly over his chest.

"Daddy?" Alice asked.

John looked at her through a haze and noticed

the wild look in her eyes. Alice had followed Alexa's order and hadn't finished herself off.

"Can I cum now?" She asked. Alice was squirming uncomfortably, her pussy glistening with her moisture, coating her thighs and pooling beneath her.

"You've been such a perfect girl, Alie," he said. His cock was still hard and twitching, cum dribbling from the head. Alexa had pushed John over the edge, but the build-up had been so much that his cock was still hard. Alice was drunk with lust and edging.

"Come here, baby girl," John said, stroking his wet cock.
Alice crawled her way over to him, licking her lips as she watched his hand tug on his shaft. She stopped in front of him, still on her hands and knees.

"Stay just like that," he said, getting on his knees behind her.
Alice obeyed, glancing over her shoulder at him as he positioned himself behind her. Alice was shivering in anticipation. A surprised yelp

escaped her lips when John tugged lightly on the tail of the butt plug that was still inside of her ass. Alice moaned as her body burned for him.

"Please, Daddy." John wrapped the fur of the tail around his forearm, gently tugging on it, eliciting soft whimpers of pleasure from his little girl. Alexa lay on the carpet, watching them, enjoying the sight. She was spent, her body tingling from her orgasms and her headlight. He thrust his cock into Alice's waiting pussy and groaned as a new wave of pleasure rocked him. Alice pushed back against him, letting his cock fill her, gently wiggling herself onto his cock as she adjusted to his size. She began rocking against him, causing the length of the tail to tighten and release rhythmically around his arm. Alice was filled to the brim, unable to control herself anymore. After a moment, letting Alice set the rhythm, John matched her speed. He made long, slow thrusts as Alice gyrated against him. She let herself go, her body relaxing, taking his cock as deep as it could go. Her ass was filled with the butt plug that John tugged on to remind her that it was still there. Not that she needed the reminder. With the length of the tail wrapped around his forearm, every thrust reminded her, and the smallest movement sent a shock of pleasure through her ass and pussy. The sensations built upon each other and set her heart beating rapidly as her desire grew with each thrust.

"Faster," Alice said, too delirious to form full sentences. Her breathing was fast, and her head swam with thoughts of her Daddy pounding his cock deep into her dripping pussy. John grinned at her quiet request. He increased his speed a little with each thrust, not wanting her to reach her orgasm too quickly. Alice was whimpering, clawing at the carpet, by the time Alexa had collected herself. She was watching the two of them from the sidelines, blissful and satisfied, their combined scent clinging to her skin.

"Tell Daddy what you want, Alie. Tell Daddy how much you want him," Alexa said, rolling onto her side, lazily stroking herself.

John's cock swelled and throbbed inside Alice's pussy as he listened to her moan and pant. He kept his pace steady, drawing out her pleasure as she stretched her arms out in front of her, pressing her breasts into the floor, arching her back.

"Please." It was all Alice could get out. Her mind was flooded with lust and desire, only focusing on one thing.

"I want you to fuck me, Daddy," Alice said. John increased his pace, and Alice's answering grunt told him she was close. He thrust into her, her pussy stroking his cock and tightening around his shaft with each quick thrust. Alice's eyes closed as her pleasure stacked. She was so close that if he stopped right now, she would burst into tears.

"Fuck!" Alice screamed as she finally came. Her body twitched violently, her pussy tightening around his cock and her ass doing the same with the butt plug. Her scream turned into loud whimpers. Her eyes closed, and her breathing was ragged.

John kept his rhythm as Alice tightened around his cock. Her pleasure warmed him, causing a familiar feeling in his balls. He was gasping for breath, sweat beading on his brow.

Alice moaned again as her orgasm slowly tapered out, and John pulled his cock in and out of her twitching pussy, loving the feel of her body's pleasure. He pulled himself out, and Alice moaned in protest. John chuckled and thrust back in, taking her hard and fast, fucking her until he thought of nothing but finishing inside of her wet, tight pussy. John grunted, forcing himself to pull out seconds before he came. Hot streams of cum spurted over her ass and back, matting into the fur of the tail.

John swayed behind her, slowly stroking the last few drops of his cum from his cock.

Alice moaned in satisfaction, stretching herself out on her belly. John lay down next to her, trailing a hand over her back, drawing circles on her skin, raising goosebumps in his wake. Alexa scooted closer, sandwiching their little girl between them. She kissed her nose and pushed

Alice's dark, wild hair from her face. Her cheeks were flushed, and her eyes glazed over, a soft smile on her lips, and there was a hint of a dimple in her cheek.

"I think we should get cleaned up, don't you?" Alexa said, and Alice giggled.

"But I'm sleepy," she said.

"I know, baby girl." Alexa murmured, lacing her fingers through Alice's.

Alice reluctantly sat up. She took Alexa's offered hand and rose to her feet slowly, her head feeling as though it was tenuously filled with helium and attached to her neck by a string. Her pussy was still twitching, and her legs weak as she gingerly took a step. Her head swirled dizzyingly, and Alexa caught her, laughing.

"S'not funny," Alice mumbled, but she smiled despite herself.

"Of course you are, baby girl. You're the funniest and the sweetest," Alexa said and kissed her cheek.

＊＊＊

Alexa got into the tub with her and hugged her close as the warm water soaked into them. Their scent mingled with the fruity aroma of the bubble bath Alice had chosen. Alexa combed her fingers through the ends of Alice's hair.

"That's nice," Alice said sleepily.

"Did you have fun, Alie?" Alexa asked.

"Yes, Mommy. Did I do good?"

"You did well, baby. You were such a good girl." Alice grinned, "Really?"

"Really," Alexa confirmed, and she kissed the top of her dark hair. The buns had come undone, and the ribbons were hanging limply. Alexa gently untied the knots and set the ribbons on the edge of the tub.

"Can we have ice cream later?" Alice asked as Alexa brushed her fingers through her hair again.

"Of course, but only after dinner."

"Aw," Alice said, pulling a face and sticking her tongue out.

"You know the rules, baby," Alexa said,

smiling softly.

"I know, Mommy."

"Can we watch cartoons while we eat?" Alice asked after a few moments.

"Yes, we can," Alexa said and snuggled her face into Alice's neck. Alice giggled and hugged Alexa's arms to her breast.

"I had fun today, Mommy," Alice said.

"I'm so happy to hear that, baby girl. I had fun, too."

"I'm glad that I met you and Daddy," Alice said, turning her head so she could nuzzle Alexa's neck. Alexa smiled, Alice's words making her heart thump in her chest. Alice scooted forward in the bath and handed the bottle of bath gel to Alexa. "Can you help me wash my back, please?" Alexa grabbed the gel, and the giant strawberry-shaped sponge Alice had picked out. The gel made a generous lather, and Alexa gently scrubbed Alice's skin.

"Stand up," Alexa said. "But be careful. Use the support bar."

"Okay, Mommy." Alice stood, glad for the

non-slip mat that Alexa had put in just for her. The bath oils Alice had bought on a whim were notorious for making the tub a slippery bowl of death. Alexa gently scrubbed between Alice's legs, running down the inner thigh and back up again in small circles. Alice shivered, cooling down from their play.

"I think we should make waffles for dessert," Alice said, already thinking of covering the whole thing in ice cream and caramel syrup.

***

"Daddy!" Alice squealed. She bounced towards him in the kitchen where he had dinner prepared and was setting the table, her koala tucked under her arm.

"Careful, baby girl. This stuff's hot."

"What did you make, Daddy?" Alice asked, toning down her excitement and plopping into a kitchen chair. She dropped her head in her palms and watched as he set out serving spoons and a huge bowl of salad.

"Cottage pie," Alice happily clapped her hands together. The jostling made Beanie fall from her arms. Alice's robe was slightly too big for her, the sleeves covering her hands. She flapped them and giggled again. She was sleepy and very, very comfortable. She carefully hopped off the chair and collected her koala, setting him in his chair.

"Daddy, can I make a place for Beanie?" Alice asked.

"Yes, you can, but wait for me to help you, okay?"

"Okay, Daddy," Alice said, still flapping her one, sleeved arm like a lopsided little bird.

***

Alice pulled John by the hand to the small table in the corner of her room. Alexa leaned in the doorway, watching over them, her heart light.

"Don't stay up too late, Alie," she said and gave John a meaningful look and pointed at her watchless wrist.

"Don't let her sweet-talk her way into an extra hour, or you'll be in trouble, too." Alexa winked and left them to their fun. Alexa had some work to tend to before Monday and didn't want to do it tomorrow while Alice was awake.

"Yes, Mommy." Alice fluffed up her pillow and dropped into it.
John followed suit less gracefully. "What do you want to do?"

"This!" Alice said and pulled a medium-sized box from the shelf beside her, setting it on the table. It was filled with multi-colored blobs of clay and playdough wrapped in cling wrap or stuffed into ziplock bags. Alice turned the box over, dumping the contents onto the table. After a few minutes of rummaging through the packages, she huffed, "I'm out of green."

"What do you want to use green for?" John asked.

"I wanted to make grass." Alice pouted.

"Well, there's a little trick I learned when I took a semester of art theory in college," John said and grabbed a big pinch of yellow and one blue. When he squashed the two colors together, Alice let out a yelp of surprise.

"No! No, Daddy! I'm not allowed to mix them!" Her voice was high and shrill, genuinely panicked.

"Don't worry, baby girl. I'm helping you so that Mommy won't get mad."

Alice frowned, "But…" John cocked his head at her and pulled a funny face, "If Daddy says it's okay, Mommy won't get mad, baby."

"Okay, Daddy," she said.

John showed her how to mix the two different colors well so that they didn't make swirly yellow and blue streaks in random spots, adding in a little bit of blue to make it a shade or so darker. When he was done, there was a light green tint to the palm of his hands, and Alice laughed.

"Here you go, Alie," John said proudly. Alice took the lump from him and inspected it.

"Good job, Daddy," Alice said, nodding her head. She rolled the clump of green clay into a long thin snake, showing her Daddy how to make sure it was even all over, breaking off pieces when they were just the right thickness and length to pass as grass. Every so often, Alice stopped to inspect John's handiwork, nodding, and letting him continue. When she was satisfied that there were enough little green bits, she showed him how and where to place the little blobs of clay-grass on the wooden board she was using for her sculpture. They did end up staying up *way* past her bedtime, but John and Alice had managed to finish their happy little diorama.

"This is you," Alice said. "This one is Mommy."

"Where are you?" John asked, peeking around the back of the small, lopsided house.

"Over here, silly." Alice giggled and pointed out her clay stickman standing right in the middle of the two giant people that towered over the house.

"Oh, now I see! You did such a good job, baby girl."

Alice threw her arms around him and crawled into his lap, yawning.

"Thank you for playing with me," Alice

said. John wrapped her in a tight hug, "Any time, baby girl." He gently rocked her, humming her favorite song, listening as her breathing changed and she fell asleep in his arms.

Who is Tina Moore?

Tina Moore has enjoyed the lifestyle of a Mommy Domme for several years. She began secretly exploring kink and BDSM in her youth and found her love of being a strict Mommy Domme in early 2000. Tina Moore slowly became more comfortable and confident through making friends in the community and exploring the lifestyle and now openly celebrates being a Mommy Domme to her little.

Before becoming an author, Tina Moore worked in the finance sector, but it was through the encouragement of her current little that she took the leap and wrote her first MDLG book, Nancy's Little One.

From then on, Tina Moore continued to combine her experiences and desires, as well as the sweet and naughty things her baby girl does, to bring you tantalizing and salacious stories about both MDLG and DDLG relationships and the ABDL littles and middles who enjoy them.

Follow her on:

Author Page on Amazon

Instagram @tinamoore.kdp